THE BARON'S HALO

The Welwyn Marriage Wager
Book 2

By
Jenna Jaxon

Text by Jenna Jaxon
Cover by Kim Killion Designs

Dragonblade Publishing, Inc. is an imprint of Kathryn Le Veque Novels, Inc.
P.O. Box 23
Moreno Valley, CA 92556
ceo@dragonbladepublishing.com

Produced in the United States of America

First Edition September 2023
Trade Paperback Edition

ARE YOU SIGNED UP FOR DRAGONBLADE'S BLOG?

You'll get the latest news and information on exclusive giveaways, exclusive excerpts, coming releases, sales, free books, cover reveals and more.

Check out our complete list of authors, too!

No spam, no junk. That's a promise!

Sign Up Here

www.dragonbladepublishing.com

Dearest Reader;

Thank you for your support of a small press. At Dragonblade Publishing, we strive to bring you the highest quality Historical Romance from some of the best authors in the business. Without your support, there is no 'us', so we sincerely hope you adore these stories and find some new favorite authors along the way.

Happy Reading!

CEO, Dragonblade Publishing

Additional Dragonblade books by Author Jenna Jaxon

The Welwyn Marriage Wager Series
Until I'm Safe in Your Arms (Book 1)
The Baron's Halo (Book 2)

The Lyon's Den Series
Pride of Lyons

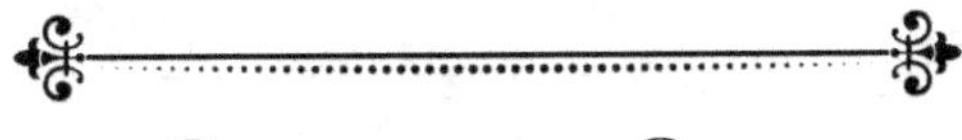

Chapter One

London
September 7, 1860

Lively waltz music filled the air in Lady Winslow's elegant ballroom, punctuated by laughter and the soft chatter of the *ton*. The light of hundreds of reflected candles gave a warm ambiance to the cream-colored fabric walls festooned with garlands of ivy dotted with little pink flowers. Saunders MacKay, Baron MacKay of Carnwath strolled around the well-appointed room, his gaze darting from young ladies dancing, to young ladies conversing, to young ladies flirting with gentlemen who looked either eager or bored by their gambits. Saunders, Sandy to his friends and relations, sighed and assumed a pleasant smile. Quite soon, he suspected, he'd be part of one of those flirting couples himself.

Sandy had remained in London after his grandfather, the Duke of Welwyn, had called him and five of his cousins all together and set them a very lucrative wager. If all six of the Quartermain cousins could manage to marry within the year, each one would receive ten thousand pounds and an estate of their choosing with all the trimmings. A wager too good for any of them to turn down, as wagers to a Quartermain were as tantalizingly irresistible as a mouse steeped in catnip was to a hungry feline. Now, Sandy and four of his cousins were attending every ball, musical evening, soiree, card party, and theatre party available in the hopes of holding up their part in the wager.

Their sixth cousin, Captain Alexander Bancroft, had already made good on his side wager to be the first to marry. He and his bride, a Miss Emma Washer, had tied the knot just last week and were now enjoying wedded bliss—at least Sandy hoped it was wedded bliss after a whirlwind courtship that had lasted a single weekend—in London while awaiting Alex's orders for his next military posting.

A quick perusal of the ballroom told him he'd have no competition from his cousins this evening. They'd likely not received entree to this élite entertainment. Lady Winslow's ball, which opened the Little Season every September, was the most sought after invitation in London. Only a select one hundred and fifty members of the *ton* were invited. And as Sandy's mother, who had been a Quartermain before her marriage, was a particular friend of Lady Winslow, he'd been granted access to a bevy of young ladies who might very well fill the bill of wife.

Thankfully, his mother was of a mind to help him win the marriage wager, not necessarily for the prize it would bring him but, as she had told him frankly, it was time she had grandchildren she could brag about. Ever since his father's untimely death in a hunting accident five years ago, Mama had been in poor spirits, roaming the castle up in Scotland like a distracted Lady Macbeth. If giving her grandchildren would lift her spirits, then it was the least Sandy could do to accommodate her.

Scanning the room once more for an unpartnered lady, Sandy could spy not one unattended. Perhaps he should consult Mother now about the young ladies whose mothers she was acquainted with and beg an introduction or two. They had discussed strategies for finding him a wife after Alex's wedding, but Sandy hadn't paid much attention. There were too many delights in London to distract his thoughts and as Mama had prattled on about this and that young lady, Sandy's mind had wandered to the much more pleasurable charms of a certain opera singer he'd taken an interest in after attending a performance of *La Traviata* earlier in the summer. Miss Theodosia Bradshaw had big blue eyes, golden hair, and the voice of a songbird. Sandy had lost himself in the lady's allures for more than a month since the summer, to the immense satisfaction of them both.

Now, however, it was autumn and if he wanted to do his part to win that wager, he needed to turn his mind from the delightful Theodosia and concentrate it on the chaste and otherwise boring young ladies of the *ton*. Mama was a stickler for the proprieties, and so he must be circumspect now, no matter how much he longed for the arms of Theodosia. Mama's sense about the worthiness of the young ladies out in Society and their suitability for marriage could not be matched. She'd arranged several marriages for his older Quartermain cousins and each of those had found her suggestions a perfect match. He only hoped Mama's senses worked equally well for her own progeny.

He glanced about the room once more, searching for his mother, when an odd movement on the dance floor drew his attention. It took a moment to discern which couple had caught his eye but in the end it turned out to be Lord Barclay. A more offensive gentleman could not be found in all the *ton*. More cad than gentleman, but with the title of a marquess and the heir to the Duke of Alderton, he was unfortunately given cart blanche with the ladies. Curling his lip in disgust, Sandy was about to return his attention to finding his mother, when his gaze met that of Barclay's partner, the loveliest young lady he'd ever seen but never met. Had he been introduced to this enchanting creature, Sandy would be the one waltzing with her this instant, not that cad Barclay.

The lady's gown, of some sort of white sheer fabric shot with blue streaks and edged in lace, while lovely, wasn't the first stare of fashion. Neither was her hair styled in a spectacular manner, although the rich, dark brunette locks that framed her face made her complexion pale to the approved shade of white. Not that any of that mattered a jot to Sandy.

Her face simply took his breath away.

Wide blue eyes the color of a fine summer's day, with sooty brows above them creased into a slight frown. Her skin was pale with a translucence that was breathtaking. Her cheeks seemed to have drawn all the color from the rest of her face, settling it onto two brilliant pools of color. He'd swear it came from the spritely exercise of dancing and not a rouge pot. She looked too natural to have any bit of artifice. That burst of vivid pink gave her a vibrancy that tantalized Sandy. Her current partner towered over her, but Sandy could imagine in his own arms she'd come exactly up to his shoulder. The perfect height for him to kiss her pink Cupid's bow mouth.

Mesmerized, Sandy stood gawking at the couple, uncaring if he was being beastly rude or not. Finally, Lord Somersby appeared at his side.

"You might wish to disguise your interest in Miss Devereaux a trifle, MacKay. People with more time on their hands than sense love to talk about such things. Don't want to appear in the latest gossip over tomorrow morning's breakfast table. The Little Season is rife with such talk." His friend grinned at him and deliberately stood in front of Sandy, shielding his view of the enchanting creature and breaking the spell the young lady had cast on him.

"Miss Devereaux, you say?" Sandy hadn't heard the name before. "Is she just out this year? I've not seen her before." How could he ever forget that face?

"Yes, since the spring. Made her curtsy to the queen and all that." Somersby peered over Sandy's head, presumably at Barclay and Miss Devereaux. "She's a shy little thing. I danced with her a time or two and she's a sweet girl, but with a strange air of sadness about her."

"Sadness?" That did sound odd. "Perhaps she was sad to have to partner you, old chap." His jest hid a sharp curiosity about Miss Devereaux now.

Somersby groaned at the quip. "I suspect she might still be mourning her father, Ambrose Grey, captain of the *Cordelia*."

"She went down three years ago, didn't she?" Sandy shivered. A watery death sounded like a terrible way to die, with all the fishes nibbling on you.

"Yes, ghastly business." His friend moved so Sandy could see Miss Devereaux once more. "She was a pleasant partner all the same, but I've had my eye on Lady Millicent Fauntleroy ever since we met in June."

Grinning, Sandy slapped Somersby on the shoulder. "When's the announcement coming out in the *Times*, old chap?"

Somersby shook his head. "No time soon, unfortunately. I'm afraid Millicent is leading me a merry chase. She can't seem to make up her mind between me and Darlington." His friend glared at someone over Sandy's head. "Bloody Darlington of all people."

Sandy turned to find the aforesaid rival laughing with Lady Millicent, who looked bewildered with all the attention. Poor Somersby. He looked fit to be tied, glaring at Darlington, shifting from foot to foot, as though he might need to find a water closet soon. That or he'd take a flyer at Darlington and make him cop a mouse.

"Steady, old chap. You won't win Lady Millicent's regard by thrashing your rival. Focus on the lady herself." Sandy felt somewhat a hypocrite dispensing such advice without ever having experienced the emotion of love. Still, he did have opinions about how a courtship could be accomplished without the worst of everyone's advice being taken. "If you do that and let it be known that the other gentleman's attentions to her mean nothing to you, Lady Millicent will come to understand you care about her, and she will appreciate you all the more."

Lady Millicent could not find a better gentleman to wed than Somersby. Sandy only hoped the lady came to that same conclusion sooner rather than later.

"Thank you, MacKay. I'll take that advice this moment if

you'll excuse me." Somersby nodded and straightened his shoulders, with a movement that seemed to be girding himself for battle. He strode over to where Lady Millicent stood chatting with her partner at the side of the dance floor.

Blast! The dance had ended while Sandy had been meddling with Somersby's troubles and now he stood staring at nothing when he'd meant to beg an introduction to Miss Devereaux from someone—anyone as long as they knew the young lady. In a panic, Sandy scanned the dance floor and discovered Miss Devereaux in conversation with Barclay. Why the hell was she still with that scoundrel? Well, he'd put a stop to that this instant. He'd be damned if he'd let that rogue finagle a second dance from the lady.

Sandy had just started across the dance floor, searching frantically for Lady Winslow who must, of course, know the young lady, when Miss Devereaux jerked back from Barclay, as if he had suddenly caught fire. She snatched her hand from his and stumbled backward abruptly, her wide-eyed gaze scanning the room, telegraphing a plea for help. Barclay too seemed startled by her action, for he stood unmoving, his hand still suspended in the air after her abrupt withdrawal.

In the seconds it took Sandy to comprehend what was happening, he'd already shoved past a group of gentlemen at the edge of the floor, dodged this way and that through the couples who were quitting the dance floor, all of whom seemed to be coming straight at him, and finally broke into an outright run. He fetched up at Miss Devereaux's side in less time than it took to breathe deeply, although it seemed as though he'd been trudging through quicksand for an hour.

Startled, the lady let out a slight "Awp," and jumped back further, as though being beset from another front.

Barclay's brows shot up, then slowly dipped into a dark frown. The scowl did nothing to improve the man's appearance. He opened his mouth, but Sandy leaped into the fray, turning to the lady, who still looked wary.

"Miss Devereaux, I believe this next set belongs to me." Sandy stared at the frightened lady, hoping to convey his good intentions through his steadfast gaze and eager smile. He couldn't have been mistaken about her dislike of something Lord Barclay had done. She'd been backing away from the man when he arrived. But she might be willing to forgive a transgression in a man she knew instead of acknowledging one she didn't know. As they had not been introduced, she'd be within her rights to wave him off. If she denied him, however, he'd be at a loss as to how to proceed.

"I was about to take Miss Devereaux back to her mother, MacKay," Barclay declared, impatience in his gravelly voice. "If you will excuse—"

"Were you indeed?" Sandy managed to put as much doubt into his tone as he dared. He glanced pointedly at the verandah door, where he suspected Barclay had been attempting to abscond with her. Well, he'd take care of that little scheme forthwith. He grinned widely into Barclay's pinched face. "Then I've saved you the effort, haven't I?"

Pursing his lips, Barclay seemed about ready to speak then, taking Sandy's fixed gaze into consideration, turned to the lady. "Would you like for me to escort you, Miss Devereaux? I am more than willing to return you to your mother."

The lady looked up at him, the frightened look smoothing out until she managed a small smile. "Thank you, Lord Barclay, but as my next partner is here, there is no need. I suspect a new set will be forming by the time we reach Mama." She looked pointedly at Sandy's arm and he hastily offered his elbow which she looped her arm through. "My thanks for a lovely waltz, my lord."

The unexpected thrill of her touch made Sandy's heart race. Beads of sweat popped out on his forehead. Thank God the room was warm enough to account for that, although he understood the heat came from within himself, not from the myriad bodies pressed together around them in the ballroom. It was all due to the petite woman now standing very close beside him, clutching his arm.

"Very well, Miss Devereaux." His smile turned into a snarl. "MacKay."

Sandy bowed, not wanting to hide his triumphant smile. "Barclay."

The young lord huffed away, leaving Sandy suddenly alone with the entrancing Miss Devereaux. But what the devil was he going to do with her? The obvious thing rose to mind. "Miss Devereaux, would you like for me to return you to your mother?"

With a slight shake of her head, she steered them toward the doors of the verandah. "No, thank you…is it Lord MacKay?"

Mesmerized by the lady, Sandy managed a nod.

A frown marred her features. "I am sorry, but have we been introduced?" Her gaze continued to hold him. "I'm certain I would remember you."

He prayed fervently that was true. Taking a deep breath, Sandy launched forth into his best version of an explanation for his bold actions. "Unfortunately not, Miss Devereaux, although I tried very hard to find Lady Winslow to ask her to introduce me to you. I was unsuccessful in that endeavor, so I must beg your pardon for my intrusion."

Sandy hesitated. He'd been certain the lady was frightened of Barclay when he barged in between them, but now he began to doubt himself. Still, he must continue with the explanation. "I thought I noted you were in some distress from Lord Barclay's proximity to you. A fictional dance set looked to be the best way to release you from his company." He stopped and stared down into her perfect blue eyes. "If I was mistaken in the nature of your exchange, I am truly sorry for interrupting your private conversation."

Miss Devereaux gave a furtive glance toward the dance floor, where the next set was indeed forming. She straightened her shoulders, then looked into his face, a determined look on her own. "Did you wish to dance this set with me, my lord?"

Catching his breath at the thought of having this lovely creature in his arms even for a few moments, Sandy smiled at her. "I would be forever grateful to be allowed to stand up with you, Miss Devereaux." He peered into her face as it went from hopeful to despairing. "However, my desires are of no consequence at the moment. I will gladly forfeit that joy in order to do whatever you bid me do."

At that, she gave him a trembling but genuine smile. "Then please take me out onto the verandah before my real partner discovers where I am and claims me."

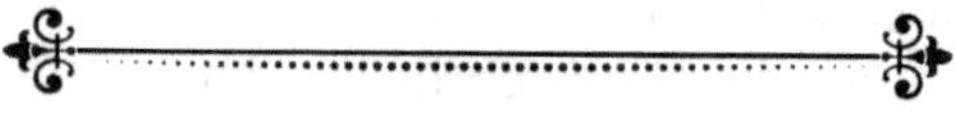

CHAPTER TWO

QUIVERING, THOUGH SHE tried her best to stop, Isabelle regretted her words to Lord MacKay almost immediately. The gentleman was a total stranger. They hadn't even been introduced properly and here she was allowing him to take her out onto a secluded verandah where who knew what liberties he might try to take with her. Still, if she didn't get out of the stifling ballroom she might run screaming through Lady Winslow's house out into the night.

Her waltz with Lord Barclay had been a dreadful mistake. She prayed her request to Lord MacKay wasn't another one.

Clenching her teeth as she remembered the feeling of Lord Barclay's hands squeezing her waist tightly during the dance, she swallowed quickly before her gorge could rise. She had to get out of here now. "Can we leave, please?"

"Of course." Without another word, Lord MacKay led her toward the verandah doors, her current hope of heaven. She danced impatiently as he cast a glance over the ballroom, then hesitated. Leaning slightly toward her, he laughed then whispered, "Not yet. Lady Marksby is looking this way."

Thank goodness for her escort's cool head. Lady Marksby's sharp eyes had ruined more than one young lady's reputation.

"Now, go." He opened the French doors just wide enough so her hoops could glide through them, then she was out in the night and its blessedly cool air.

Isabelle breathed as deeply as her tightly laced corset would allow, and a measure of calm descended on her. Here in the semi-darkness, she could convince herself that she was safe, that no one would harm her. She glanced at her escort, apprehension rising once more, but he made no move toward her. Still, caution won out and she retreated from him, putting several feet of distance between them and putting her into the shadows beyond the illumination of the overhead lanterns.

"Did Barclay hurt you in any way, Miss Devereaux?"

Isabelle couldn't see Lord MacKay's face, but the menace in his voice came through clear as day. She needed to tread carefully with this unknown entity. "Why no, my lord. Why would you think that?"

"Because of the way you jerked away from him just now, after the dance."

Curse the man for having sharp eyes. She shouldn't have been so obvious, but when Lord Barclay's hand had strayed to her waist and she'd felt the pressure of him pulling her toward him, she'd reacted without rational thought. For him to have done it during the dance had been bad enough. To repeat the offense while they were conversing afterward, when anyone could see the liberty—had seen it, apparently—had been too much to bear. "It was nothing, my lord. I…I should not have been so…hasty."

"Indeed?" Lord MacKay strode forward into the light, his face now clearly visible in the lantern's glow. It was an arresting face, handsome as a chiseled stone had beauty in its stark planes. Jet black hair glinted coldly in the soft light. His dark eyes under darker brows rested unwaveringly on her. "I must disagree with you, Miss Devereaux. I believe Lord Barclay took egregious liberties with you, both on and off the dance floor."

"And why would you think that, my lord?" Oh, she should never have come out here with Lord MacKay. Should never have agreed to dance with Lord Barclay. Should never have come to Lady Winslow's ball at all.

"Because I know Lord Barclay to be a cad of the most dangerous kind."

"What kind is that?"

"A gentleman with a title that makes matchmaking mamas overlook his lack of decency in the hopes of securing him and his position for their daughters." Lord MacKay's stare bore into her. "Did you accept a dance with him because you wished to do so, or was it at the urging of your mother perhaps?"

Isabelle hung her head. "My mother suggested it. She wishes me settled this year." Which was nothing out of the ordinary in Polite Society. Raising her head, she stared back at Lord MacKay. "There is nothing inappropriate in dancing with a gentleman."

"Inappropriate, no. Ill-advised yes, especially when the man in question has no respect whatsoever for women." He drew himself up, as if about to make a formal declaration. "Did Lord Barclay insult you with attentions that are considered beyond the pale, Miss Devereaux?"

"If he did do so, my lord, there is nothing that can be done about it now." Her words came out sharper than intended, but Lord MacKay seemed to be bordering on impertinence himself.

"On the contrary, Miss Devereaux, if you tell me he engaged in indecent behavior toward you, it will be my pleasure to call the scoundrel out."

Isabelle's breath caught in her throat. "Call him out?"

"In a duel for your honor." Lord MacKay looked deathly serious.

"But…but dueling isn't done. Not anymore." He would champion her in such a manner when they hadn't even been properly introduced? Isabelle's head spun. It was either the most foolhardy or the most romantic thing she'd ever heard. "And it can't be legal."

He shrugged, keeping his gaze firmly on her. "A mere technicality. That would not deter me in the least from seeking satisfaction from such a cad."

Gracious, the gentleman was serious. He actually meant to

fight Lord Barclay. She must put a stop to the notion this instant. The ensuing scandal would, without a doubt, ruin her forever. "I assure you, my lord, such an action is not necessary, although I thank you for your chivalry."

"I deem it the greatest honor, Miss Devereaux, to be at your service in whatever capacity you find a need." Lord MacKay's intense gaze continued to hold hers, leaving her quite breathless. The earnestness in his deep voice made her heart stutter.

A sudden gust of wind sent a chill through Isabelle, reminding her that they had been outside for too long.

"Allow me at least to demonstrate my service to you, albeit in a much more trivial way."

Before she could protest, he had whipped off his jacket and draped it around her shoulders. A hint of citrus cologne immediately enveloped her, a somehow comforting fragrance. The heavy garment, of soft dark wool, warmed her as though she stood before a friendly fire. She pulled the jacket closer, reveling in the comfort it provided her. "Thank you, my lord. You are very kind."

"Think nothing of it." His face split in a grin that changed him from somber to boyish. "I am partial to rescuing damsels in distress. Unfortunately, I am rarely able to do so here in England, although I manage it fairly often at my home in Scotland."

"Are the ladies of Scotland so often beset by cads and scoundrels?" Isabelle couldn't help but smile. "Or do you still have to deal with dragons up in the north?"

"You might be surprised, Miss Devereaux," his warm chuckle raised her spirits, "what we Scots have to put up with." He paused, his manner suddenly sober. "You make me forget that we still have not been properly introduced."

She'd forgotten also. Totally improper for them to be conversing so familiarly without a formal introduction. But it had been an unusual night all around. "Do you truly think we should stand on ceremony? If so I suppose we should return to the ballroom. Lady Winslow will be able to make the introductions if we can find her." Still, she was loathe to leave the comfort of the verandah and the solace of Lord MacKay's company. "Is that what you desire, my lord?"

"As I said earlier, Miss Devereaux, my desires matter not at all. But if you wish to remain outside here, may I suggest you permit me to introduce myself." He drew himself up, then clicked his heels and bowed low before her. "Saunders MacKay, Baron MacKay of Carnwath in Scotland, at your devoted service."

Biting back a giggle, Isabelle curtsied deeply to him. Turn about was fair play after all. "A Scottish baron." That sounded so romantic. "I am so pleased to meet you, my lord. Allow me to introduce myself as well. Miss Isabelle Devereaux."

"Enchanted, Miss Devereaux." He grasped her hand and bent over it. The barest graze of his lips on the fabric of her glove brought a wave a heat all the way to Isabelle's head.

Oh, dear. And now she was here alone with him and feeling so…warm, despite the chilly wind. Isabelle shook her head to clear it. They should go back inside. Sooner or later they would be missed and that could prove disastrous.

Also, she must find and apologize to Mr. Bufkin for her abominably rude behavior. He had been promised her next dance and the gentleman had likely scoured the ballroom in search of his partner. Perhaps he could be placated with the promise of another set, although he might not now wish to partner her if he felt he'd been snubbed. The rules of etiquette were strict and people took offence to the smallest infractions. But if a young lady wished to be out in Society to find a husband, she had to abide by the rules or risk the life of a spinster.

A fate Isabelle fervently wished for. Despite her mother's instructions on how to secure a husband, thoughts of marriage brought disturbing images to Isabelle's mind. Her mother's marriage to her father had been happy, but memories of that long ago time did nothing to persuade her to wish for marriage.

"Is something the matter, Miss Devereaux?"

Lord MacKay's deep voice startled her out of her reverie.

"Not at all, my lord." She gazed up at him, struck once more by his rugged good looks that seemed oddly paired with his gentle nature. Of course, he had offered to kill Lord Barclay, so obviously he had a harsher side to him as well. But he'd been nothing but kind to her. "I was woolgathering, I'm afraid."

"A pleasant pastime, to be sure. One I wish we could indulge in at some length." A smile flitted over his lips. "However, as your newly acquired champion, I fear I must advise you to return to the ballroom before someone comes looking for you. I would not wish to save you from one compromising situation only to land you in another one."

"Not even if you were the one to compromise me, Lord MacKay?" The teasing whisper in the back of her mind had suggested that very thing as soon as they had come out onto the verandah. Isabelle had hushed the voice during most of their conversation out here, but still the idea lingered. It was difficult for her to trust any gentleman. Even a man sworn to champion her.

"Not even then, Miss Devereaux." His face had reverted to its stern lines, with the addition of pursed lips, that gave it the ring of truth. "I would never wish to so dishonor any woman, but especially not you."

Isabelle liked him all the better for that sentiment. And strangely, she believed him, despite not knowing him much at all. She nodded. "Then let us go in by all means. As you say, we shall be missed and likely sooner rather than later."

She started for the French doors, but his hand on her arm stopped her.

"I think I must retrieve my jacket first, Miss Devereaux." His eyes glinted in the dim lighting, a wide smile showing his white teeth.

Dear Lord! Had she appeared in Lord MacKay's clothing there would have been nothing that could have stopped the scandal. Isabelle shrugged out of the garment and shivered as the chill wind buffeted her exposed shoulders. She missed its warmth and the connection it had given her to its rightful owner.

Lord MacKay pulled the jacket on, smoothed it down with a practiced hand, and offered his arm. "Now we may proceed." He stopped with his hand on the door's latch. "May I ask for an introduction to your mother?"

Somehow the request made her heart flutter. "Of course, my lord. She will be happy to see I have found another gentleman I wish to stand up with."

"You sound as though that were a miraculous thing." He opened the door and they stepped back into the overly warm ballroom.

"It is, I assure you." Isabelle immediately searched for her mother and noted she'd not changed her position. Still speaking to Lady Dalrymple, just as Isabelle had left her at least half an hour ago. She sighed. A more vigorous gossip did not exist in London.

"Then you are granting me a dance this evening?"

Her attention flew back to Lord MacKay, still at her side. His voice held a note of excitement that in turn sent a thrill down Isabelle's back. "As you announced it to Lord Barclay, I think we must keep our word. I would not wish to provoke the man into calling you a liar."

"Barclay can go hang, but if it gains me a dance with you, Miss Devereaux, then I am the happiest man in Christendom." He perused the room. "Which lady is your mother?"

"There," Isabelle nodded, "the one in the maroon gown speaking with Lady Dalrymple."

"I see we are not going to escape being as least a footnote to gossip tomorrow. Here," he tucked her arm securely into the crook of his elbow. "If it were done, 'twas best 'twere done quickly."

They strolled swiftly toward Mama, Isabelle hoping against hope that Lady Dalrymple would take herself off before they reached her, but of course when she saw them headed toward Mama, the older lady fixed them with a knowing look and waited eagerly as they approached.

"Hello, Mama. Good evening, Lady Dalrymple."

The lady took the two of them in as they stopped before her, her gaze resting solely on Lord MacKay. "Well, I see you've found a new partner, Sandy."

Isabelle's eyes widened, but she shouldn't have been surprised. Lady Dalrymple knew everyone in the *ton*.

"Well, as you will no longer stand up with me, my lady, I have had to widen the field." Lord MacKay sent the lady a flirtatious look. "I do hope you approve."

"Indeed, I do." Lady Dalrymple nodded so vigorously the brightly colored feathers on her turban threatened to take flight. She turned to Mama. "Mrs. Grey, may I introduce Lord MacKay, the tenth Baron MacKay to you? I've known him since he was born, my dear. Sandy, this is Mrs. Miranda Grey, a dear friend of mine." Like quicksilver, Lady Dalrymple turned back to Mama. "His mother is the next youngest daughter of the Duke of Welwyn. She married Baron MacKay of Carnwath, up in the wilds of Scotland."

"The wilds are rather civilized these days, my lady." Lord MacKay shot Isabelle a too innocent look that made her gasp and giggle.

"All of Scotland is wild by my standards, young man. And I have reason to know." She turned back to Isabelle's mother. "I was almost absconded with by a Highlander back in 1823. A tall, beastly man with red hair and bushy eyebrows. I still have nightmares about it every once in a while."

"I sincerely doubt he was any of my kinsmen, Lady Dalrymple." Lord MacKay tried to sound respectful, but Isabelle could tell he wanted to burst out laughing in the worst way. "We MacKays tend to have shorter statures and dark hair. And we are more respectful of women than to try to carry them off."

"A good thing you don't, young man." The lady gave an indignant sniff. "Should you attempt such a thing with Miss Devereaux I would inform your mother forthwith."

"I must admit I do plan to carry Miss Devereaux off, but only as far as the dance floor." He turned to Mama. "With your permission, Mrs. Grey?"

"Oh, yes, my lord. By all means, if dear Isabelle has agreed to partner you." Mama's resigned face had lit up at the request. Isabelle was loath to disappoint either her or Lord MacKay.

Weary beyond belief from all the tension, Isabelle summoned her socially acceptable smile. "I did grant his lordship the next dance, Mama." The set should not take long and she certainly didn't begrudge Lord MacKay his dance. But she was tired to the bone. An evening with so much tension had left her wishing to sleep for a week, but she would instead put on her pleasant smile and return some of this gentleman's kindnesses. "Shall we, my lord?"

"Yes, Miss Devereaux." His fervent gaze warmed her all over, as though he'd put his jacket back around her. "Allow me to escort you to the floor."

He offered his arm, and Isabelle was glad to have its strength to lean on as they headed for the ballroom floor. About halfway there, Lord MacKay leaned over to her, his breath warm in her ear and whispered, "Lord Barclay's eyes look ready to pop out of his head. I suppose he did think me a liar then. Pity you forbid me to call him out." Lord MacKay straightened and without missing a stride said, "I suppose I'll simply have to hold you too close during the dance and hope he has a fit of apoplexy." He grinned down at her. "You wouldn't mind me doing that in the interest of putting a stop to that social menace, would you, Miss Devereaux?"

Biting her tongue to keep from laughing out loud, Isabelle shook her head. "Behave yourself, my lord, or I'll go find Mr. Bufkin and let him put you both to shame."

They took their places in the longways set, grasped hands, and just as the music began, she gave his hand a squeeze.

His eyes flew open wide and Isabelle whispered, "Let us begin, then."

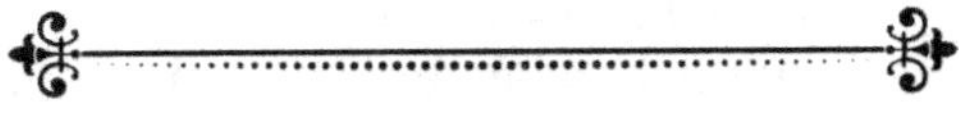

CHAPTER THREE

THE NEXT AFTERNOON Sandy headed his new curricle toward the townhouse Mrs. Grey had taken for the Little Season. Bordering on the far outskirts of Mayfair, the address wasn't the most fashionable, but Miss Devereaux's location mattered not a jot to him. If the young lady had been residing in Cheapside, he'd have been pulling up in front of that address now instead. Something about Miss Devereaux had gotten under Sandy's skin—like an itch he couldn't quite scratch—making him need to see her again as soon as possible.

When they'd left the dance floor last evening, Sandy'd been so elated, so besotted with the memory of how the lady had felt in his arms, he'd gotten all the way home before realizing he hadn't asked to call on her or request her presence on a carriage ride in Hyde Park today.

Sandy sighed in disgust as he pulled his perfectly conformed bay horse to a stop in front of a neat brick house. If he was going to be this muddle-headed about courting a young lady he needn't expect to get on very well at all. He must keep a cool head if he wished to do well during the Little Season, and especially if he wished to give Miss Devereaux a good opinion of himself. Last night's adventure had taught him the lady had hidden strengths and a cool head herself. He liked both those qualities in a woman and so hoped to pursue her long enough to assure himself she absolutely was *the one.*

Sandy had never given the idea of love at first sight any thought past its claim to be a romantic notion. No one could be so attracted to another person that quickly, or so he'd believed. Now, he found himself a possible victim of this impossible state. If it were true, he wished to be certain of his perception of the young lady and convince himself she reciprocated his feelings as well.

He wound the ribbons around the whipsocket and jumped to the pavement. Facing the front door, Sandy experienced a sudden dryness in his mouth, like he'd just swallowed sand. This was ludicrous. Even though he'd never formally called on a young lady before was no reason to panic. Such trepidation was unlike him. But what if she was out? Or refused to see him? Or saw him but refused his offer of a drive?

Head spinning from so many disastrous scenarios, Sandy stood on the pavement gazing up at the gray door with colorful stained glass outlining it. The sun winked off the plain brass doorknocker as if taunting him, daring him to knock.

"Excuse me." An older woman passed close by him, bringing Sandy back to himself.

He couldn't stand out in front of Miss Devereaux's house, blocking the pavement. Lord, how long had he been standing there? Giving himself a good shake, Sandy straightened his shoulders and mounted the short flight of stairs to the stoop. His sharp rap with the offending knocker brought a maid to the door, who showed him to a pretty parlor where Miss Devereaux and her mother sat, sipping tea and looking as though they had been waiting for him to arrive.

"Lord MacKay, ma'am." The maid curtsied, then stepped back to let him enter.

"Thank you, Dobbs." Mrs. Grey dismissed the servant, then smiled invitingly at him. "Lord MacKay, how nice to see you again. Isn't it, Isabelle?"

Sandy's attention had been riveted on Miss Devereaux from

the moment he set foot in the room. Dressed today in a white gown with tiny pink and blue flowers sprinkled generously all over it and delicate lace at the neck and cuffs, the lady reminded him of a sweetmeat ready for him to unwrap and savor all by himself.

"It is good of you to call, my lord." Miss Devereaux smiled at him and indicated a seat opposite her.

Almost bursting with the desire to be near the lady, Sandy shifted from foot to foot. "Thank you, Miss Devereaux, but I called, you see, because I forgot to ask you last night if you'd like to go for a ride with me?"

Miss Devereaux's eyes widened but she made no response.

"To Hyde Park."

Still no reply from the lady.

"In my cabriolet."

When the young lady still didn't answer, Sandy glanced at her mother for assurance that he had, indeed, been speaking. Miss Devereaux seemed lost in her thoughts so deeply Sandy didn't know if she'd heard his request or not. Did she truly need to think so long and hard about his invitation? Was his premonition that she'd refuse to ride with him about to come true?

"Isabelle." Mrs. Grey leaned over and put a hand on her daughter's arm. "Lord MacKay has invited you for a ride, my dear. Please do him the courtesy of an answer."

Miss Devereaux shook her head, as if coming out of a dream, then smiled warmly at him.

Heart racing, Sandy held his breath.

"I beg your pardon, my lord. Woolgathering again, I fear."

"That seems to be a favorite pastime." Sandy wondered just what thoughts she'd been engrossed in, but of course could not ask. "I hope driving in the park is another way you enjoy spending your time."

"I hardly know, my lord, for I've never done so before." Miss Devereaux spoke soberly, but then rose and smiled sweetly, sending a lightning bold to Sandy's heart. "But I hope to find out shortly. If you will excuse me, I'll only be a moment." The lady hurried from the room, seeming to take most of the light in the room with her.

To pass the time, Sandy engaged Mrs. Grey in conversation about various suitable topics including several entertainments she and her daughter had accepted invitations for, so the time was well spent. When Miss Devereaux returned, she was newly attired in a stunning blue and white striped carriage dress. The white jacket, embroidered around the edges with a large, bold floral pattern, draped over her arms ending in bell sleeves, and over her hoops into a short train. An ensemble certainly made to be seen by all members of the *ton*.

Sandy jumped to his feet, feeling as though he should make some remark about her stunning appearance. He feared, however, that his exuberance would make her uncomfortable, so he merely smiled enthusiastically and asked, "Are you ready to leave?"

She nodded and cast her gaze downward, twining her fingers together as though she would pull them off.

An awkward silence ensued in which Sandy tried to think how to take his leave of Mrs. Grey when he could scarcely take his eyes off her daughter. At last he simply said, "We will return shortly," then headed for the front door, hoping to God this awkwardness would soon pass.

Once Sandy had helped Miss Devereaux into his carriage and took his own place beside her, he'd gotten himself in hand. Perhaps some conversation would lighten their drive. "We have a perfect day for our drive. One is never certain what the weather will do in September."

"That is true, my lord." Her polite answer gave nothing to allow him to continue along that topic.

He waited, hoping she would produce her own conversational gambit, but after a few minutes of dreadful silence, Sandy feared he'd need to take the bull by the conversational horns. He pointed to a robin hopping bravely toward a crust of bread over in the grass in front of a passing house. "A crown says that robin gets his bread crust."

Miss Devereaux's neck turned so quickly toward him the muscles in her neck creaked. After a moment's consideration, she returned her gaze to the robin, who had indeed secured the bit of bread. "What an odd thing to place a wager on, my lord."

"Not in my family, I'm afraid. We Quartermains are all wagering fools, if I say so myself. Always have been." He turned the horses into Hyde Park and started them down Rotten Row.

"Who is 'we?'"

Excellent. He'd finally managed to pique her interest. "Currently it's myself and six of my cousins plus my grandfather actively wagering. In the past my mother and her brothers and sisters were avid wagerers as well." He leaned over conspiratorially. "I've been told my mother wagered on how quickly she could bring my father up to scratch."

"Goodness." Fortunately, Miss Devereaux didn't look scandalized in the least, merely interested. Providential on so many fronts. "And did she win?"

"Oh, she did indeed. I must let her tell you that story. It's one of her favorites." Sandy slowed the horses. Not many carriages out this afternoon despite the excellent weather, which made a slow turn around the avenue quite manageable. He wanted to spend as much time with Miss Devereaux as possible.

"Was that the only time your relatives have wagered on a marriage?" The lady cocked her head, a rapt look on her face.

He'd managed to capture her attention at last, but with perhaps the worst subject he could be talking about with her. Still, his cousin Alex had told all the remaining cousins they should be forthright about the family wager. Well, in for a penny…

"Actually, it's not. My grandfather recently set me and my cousins a marriage wager."

"A marriage wager?" Her brows dipped into a deep vee. "What does that mean?"

Taking a deep breath and sending a prayer up to a beneficent

God, Sandy launched forth into the circumstances of last month's summons, his grandfather's challenge to them all, and his cousin Alex's hasty wedding ten days later.

"By rights that should be the scandal of the Little Season, Lord MacKay." The indignation in her voice made Sandy's heart sink. "Marriage is a sacred bond, not something to be cheapened with such a thing as a wager."

"I doubt my cousin or his wife would deem their marriage cheap simply because it occurred abruptly." Well, that certainly wasn't the reaction Sandy had expected from Miss Devereaux.

The lady's brows had eased from their deep frown, however, her lips were still firm. "I did not mean to criticize your relatives, my lord." She looked uncomfortable and cast her gaze down at her lap. "Please forgive me."

"At this instance, of course, Miss Devereaux. I'm certain it seems strange to those who have not grown up in such a family." Blast. How to get the conversation back on a safer track. "And all my cousins of marriageable age know they need to begin the hunt for a wife in any case. We are at that age at which it becomes expected. Grandfather is merely giving us all a nudge. We're truly keen on the idea, well, with the exception of my cousin, Tom. Mr. Thomas Weston. He's the youngest of our set and thinks he should have his freedom a bit longer."

"Did you finally convince him to join in the wager?" Apparently, Miss Devereaux's good spirits had returned and she smiled at him.

"It took a bit of convincing from us all, but he came around eventually. Of course, Grandfather had to sweeten Tom's lot to include a ship of his own with a crew before he'd give his consent to marry at scarcely one-and-twenty. Still," Sandy turned them back toward the Hyde Park Gate and slowed the team to a walk, "now we are all actively searching for brides."

The sentence hung in the air between them for much too long.

"I don't—"

"Have you found—"

They started speaking at the same time, so of course they then both stopped talking at once.

"I beg your pardon, Lord MacKay. Please continue."

"Ladies first as always, Miss Devereaux." His curiosity must be satisfied on what she had been about to ask.

The lady's cheeks grew bright and rosy. "I merely wondered if *any* of your relations had found their prospective brides yet, my lord."

Biting back a smile, Sandy paused to consider his answer. "One of my cousins, as I said, is now married, so he has found his happiness already. The others, as far as I know, are still searching, although one cousin may have a particular young lady in mind." But her original question had sounded as though it had been directed specifically toward him. So how to address that answer without appearing too forward. "For myself, I don't quite know how to answer you. If I say yes, I have found a young lady, you might think me a cad worse than Lord Barclay for being here with you and not with her. If I say no, you might believe I am not considering you as a prospective bride." He deliberately stared into her exquisitely blue eyes, so wide they seemed to fill her face. "I would not have you believe that for a single moment."

Her entire face grew bright red, then drained to a pasty white.

Good lord, had he alarmed or offended her in some way? He gave her a minute, hoping she wouldn't swoon out here in the park.

"If you would tell me, my lord," Miss Devereaux's breathing steadied as she seemed to collect herself, her face returning to a more normal, rosy complexion. "What was the most outrageous wager you have engaged in thus far?"

The unexpected question gave Sandy pause. Possibly his most outrageous wager had involved an evening with a delectable night flower and an ostrich feather, but he certainly couldn't reveal *that* to a lady such as Miss Devereaux. Something a bit less salacious yet still extreme enough to fit the bill. God knew he'd been party to many such wagers over the years. "I believe that particular wager occurred when I was twelve years old and involved myself and several of my cousins."

"Young boys can be that shocking, my lord?" She obviously didn't believe that to be true. "I don't have any younger brothers or perhaps I wouldn't need to ask that question."

"Our family, in addition to being wagering fools, have always been inclined to be daredevils." An understatement if ever that was one. "My cousins Julius, Francis, Ulysses and I were at my grandfather's estate in Hertfordshire one summer, as I said, when I was twelve. The four of us had been swimming in the River Mimram that ran through the estate. There were several trees overhanging our swimming area and Ulysses—we call him Yule for short—the oldest of us, wagered me that I couldn't climb one of the trees."

"That doesn't seem shocking in any way, my lord." Her soft smile made Sandy's heart miss a beat.

"No, but the worst part of it was yet to come." Sandy shook his head, wondering how boys managed to survive into adulthood. "It was a willow tree which, if you do not know, is not meant for climbing at all. I had a devil of a time getting up there because the branches kept cracking and popping every time I put a foot on them."

"Goodness, my lord." Miss Devereaux looked alarmed, which was edifying considering Sandy had obviously survived. "You were quite the daredevil."

"Oh, but wait." Sandy brought the carriage to a halt just before the Hyde Park Gate. "Once I reached the specified branch and won that wager, Yule called out that he had a better wager for me. He said he'd wager I would kill myself if I jumped into the water from the tree."

"He wanted you to kill yourself!" The shock on Miss Devereaux's face matched that of his mother's when she'd found out about the exploit. "Obviously, you said no."

"Well, I was pretty high up in the tree. If I hit the ground I knew I might well have been severely injured or killed. But hitting the water, I believed I would live to win the wager." The memory of standing in there in the tree, calculating how likely his odds of surviving were was permanently etched in Sandy's memory.

"And what was the wager for, if I may ask?"

"Yule's collection of tin soldiers we'd been playing with before we'd gone swimming." Grinning at her indignant expression, Sandy shook his head. "To a twelve-year-old boy, Miss Devereaux, the game was very much worth the candle."

"Well, obviously you survived." Her smile had turned rueful.

"As you see." He motioned to himself. "I hit the water with a loud smack, leaving my chest on fire with a bright red mark on my belly. That was how my mother found out about the wager and why my grandfather took a cane to me." Literally adding insult to an already stinging injury. "I could only sleep on my side for several nights."

"But you won the set of toy soldiers?"

"I did. I have them set up in the library at my home in Carnwath, waiting for my sons to play with them."

"Hopefully, however, not to wager over?" Miss Devereaux's lips had pursed, but there weas also mirth deep within her eyes.

"Well, they will come by it honestly if they do." With a sigh, Sandy started the team again and drove them smartly out of the park. He couldn't help feeling they were speaking of their own children to come. The idea warmed his heart.

In no time they had arrived back at Miss Devereaux's townhouse. Sandy helped her down and escorted her to the door. "Thank you so much, Miss Devereaux, for allowing me to drive you this afternoon. I hope you enjoyed yourself."

"I did, Lord MacKay. Thank you for a lovely and enlightening outing." The lady smiled at him as the door opened. "I trust you will refrain from such daredevil ways before I see you again."

"I will so endeavor." Sandy gazed into her eyes, never wanting her to leave. "Will you be attending Lady Bascomb's card party tomorrow evening?"

"We will, my lord." The hint of expectation in her voice thrilled him.

"Then I hope you will allow me to partner you in some of the games." His heart beat fiercely as her gaze softened. "I think we would enjoy being partners—at whist or pique."

"I believe so too, my lord." Her smile became rueful once more. "As long as your wagers are all within reason."

"You may depend upon it, Miss Devereaux." Completely satisfied with the day's outing, Sandy bowed and left, knowing he'd be counting each hour until he could partner her at whist. And if he played his cards right, by the end of the party they'd be yet another step closer to being permanent partners.

AS ISABELLE ENTERED their foyer, she tugged at the ribbons of her bonnet and pulled it from her head, unsettled by how much she'd enjoyed her drive with Lord MacKay. She'd hoped the outing might have discouraged his interest in her—and hers in him. But she'd known when she'd put on this stunning carriage dress, his attention would be riveted on her. Oh, she'd promised Mama she'd wear it, but she could have changed into a less eye-catching ensemble and suffered her mother's censure later on. But deep down she wanted Lord MacKay to think well of her, which might make things awkward for them in the future. If only the gentleman weren't so engaging she could have put him from her mind as she'd done with the others. Now she'd gone and had a lovely time with him in spite of herself.

"Is that you, Isabelle?" Her mother's voice drew her into the parlor where her mother sat looking as though she'd not moved a muscle since Isabelle had left.

"Hello, Mama." Isabelle entered the room and went forward to kiss her mother's forehead.

The avid interest on her mother's face told Isabelle she would have to relay everything about her ride with Lord MacKay or have no peace at all this evening.

"Did you enjoy your ride with his lordship?" Eagerness filled Mama's face.

"I truly didn't expect to, but I have to admit I did." Isabelle dropped her bonnet on a nearby table. "We went to Hyde Park, of course, although there was no one there to speak of." That had seemed odd to Isabelle, although she was grateful not to have been interrupted while Lord MacKay regaled her with the tales of his wagering. The gentleman was nothing if not entertaining.

"Well, you were a bit early for the Grand Strut, unfortunately. It would have been so much better for you to have been seen going about with Lord MacKay, but I am glad you enjoyed yourselves." She looked pointedly at Isabelle. "You did make yourself agreeable company to him, didn't you, my dear?"

"I did, Mama. I truly am trying." She spun in place so her gown swirled about her. "I wore the gown as you requested, didn't I?" Her mother had bespoken the carriage gown specifically for Isabelle to wear should she be invited to drive with a gentleman. It was too singular for her tastes, but she had to admit it did catch the eye.

"I was so pleased to see it when you came down." The smile on her mother's lips held a touch of glee. "I believe Lord MacKay was quite taken with it as well. He couldn't take his eyes off you."

"Mama!" What upset Isabelle most was that she suspected Mama was correct.

"It becomes you so well. Here." Her mother patted the seat cushion next to her. "You must sit and tell me everything about your drive."

With the sigh of a martyr, Isabelle sat down as told and proceeded to disclose the particulars of their drive, down to the little details that always warmed her mother's heart, including Lord MacKay's penchant for wagers and his terrifying youthful escapades.

"Goodness, Isabelle. I hope his lordship has given up such wild ways." Mama was just pouring their second cup of tea.

"He was twelve at the time, Mama. I daresay he no longer climbs trees."

"Does he still indulge in such wild wagering?"

Isabelle sipped the soothing tea, contemplating the merits of informing her mother of Lord MacKay's current wager. It wouldn't do to get Mama's hopes up, but if—no, when she heard about the Welwyn Marriage Wager she'd know Isabelle hadn't been truthful with her and life would likely be utterly miserable for a time. "I'm not certain how wild it is, but he did inform me that his family is currently engaged in a marriage wager."

Mama stared at her, her mouth falling wide open. "A what?"

Nodding, Isabelle launched into the particulars of the wager as she remembered them, until her mother sat with a broad smile on her face.

"Oh, my dear, this is wonderful. Just think, Lord MacKay has singled you out both last night and this afternoon. This is auspicious. *Very auspicious* given his family's desire for him to marry this year." Mama clasped her hands as though she could not contain her joy. "Oh, Isabelle, just think. You could be Lady MacKay this time next year."

As much as she tried, Isabelle could not muster any enthusiasm at her mother's excited words.

Mama peered at her, some of her happiness fading. "You do like Lord MacKay, do you not, Isabelle? You seemed rather distant when you left today, although you seemed more pleased when you returned."

All at once Isabelle regretted accepting that ride today. Perhaps it was cruel to give the gentleman hope when there could be none.

"I know you said you are not ready to contemplate marriage, but might you not reconsider, Isabelle?" Her mother gripped her hands tightly. "Could you consider accepting Lord MacKay should he make an offer for you? I so want you settled in a home of your own. I am the only family you have, my dear, now that your father is gone."

"My father died years ago, Mama. When I was a very small child. You seem to forget that." That her mother had almost forgotten her first husband, Isabelle's father, was a sore spot with her.

"But Ambrose raised you as his own, my dear. He provided for you like you were his own daughter."

"He was not a very kind man, Mama. You know that." If anyone knew that, it was her mother.

Tears appeared in her mother's eyes. "Be that as it may, I do worry a great deal about you, Isabelle, for you have neither father nor step-father to protect you. Only me."

"You forget Grandmama Devereaux too, I see." It hurt abominably that her mother seemed to want to forget Isabelle's father and his family completely.

"Beatrice is still living, that is true. However, she lives so far to the north, in Carlisle, and is so infirm. I doubt she could provide a proper home for you, my dear. Certainly not one to rival the home you could have with a husband, especially one such as Lord MacKay."

Isabelle sighed. From what she had learned about Lord MacKay today, he appeared to be the least objectionable gentleman to show an interest in her. Not that many had during the Season when Mama had dragged her out into Society. Lord MacKay had shown a particular partiality for her in just two days, she couldn't deny it. Moreover, he seemed a truly good and kind gentleman, if a little wild still. And Isabelle couldn't exactly find fault with that. A little wildness every once in a while was a good thing, or so she thought.

If only she wished to marry… In such a case Isabelle would be very desirous of his attentions. "From what I know of Lord MacKay, I would say he is the most agreeable gentleman of my acquaintance. And the least objectionable as a prospective husband."

"Oh, Isabelle! I knew it. I simply knew it, my dear." Her mother burst out into the most radiant of smiles and threw her arms around her, rocking them back and forth. "I knew you could learn to love someone if you just gave yourself a little time."

"Mama, I can scarcely claim to love a gentleman whose acquaintance I made only last night." And under very suspicious circumstances, although her mother must know nothing of that.

"But you may very well come to love him in time, Isabelle. If you continue to meet him and allow your affections for him to grow...well, who knows what may happen. A Christmas wedding, perhaps."

Oh, there was no turning Mama back now.

Isabelle patted her mother's back, wondering just how far Lord MacKay's penchant for chivalry extended and whether he might need to be called upon to champion her after all.

CHAPTER FOUR

"LORD MACKAY! JUST the person I was seeking." Lady Bascomb's wispy voice had been uncharacteristically raised in order for him to hear her over the substantial din in the hallway of her elegant London townhouse.

"My lady." He bowed low. "You are looking ravishing this evening as always." The lady was well into her fifties, rather plump, and short of stature, but she was a dear friend of Sandy's mother and anything he could do to make her evening bright he was bound to do it. She did look extremely well this evening, attired in a silver gown with a silver lace overlay and a necklace of diamonds around her neck whose price would buy half of Tattersall's cattle. "I am certain you are pleased with the turnout this evening." He glanced around the rooms that led off the main hall, where he'd stationed himself to await Miss Devereaux's arrival. "You seem packed to the gills."

"Oh, yes, my lord. Quite a successful evening if I do say it myself." His hostess paused for breath. "Of course too much of a good thing can try one's soul. I was seeking you, my lord, to make up a table for whist with your cousin, Lord Boxtd and Lady Augusta Hardy. Lady Augusta had asked for you particularly."

That was an odd request. He was well acquainted with the lady, although they were not on a first name basis. His cousin Julius's plight to marry her, despite her disinterest in him, was all too familiar to Sandy. Poor Jules. He'd had quite a time of it since April with the lady leading him a merry chase. Now Sandy supposed he'd somehow end up embroiled in their courtship, if you could call it that.

Sandy sighed. All he wanted to do was wait here for Miss Devereaux to put in an appearance. However, one could not say that to one's hostess and not be considered a boor. "That sounds splendid, Lady Bascomb. If I may wait here for Miss Devereaux she can make up the fourth at our table."

"An excellent idea my lord. Your cousin and Lady Augusta are in the Egyptian room." His hostess was then distracted by Lord Fenwick, already deep in his cups, weaving through the crowded room unsuccessfully, bumping into everyone and everything.

"I'll bring the lady along as soon as she appears, my lady. If you need to tend to … anything else, I'll be fine just here."

Fenwick could be a handful, depending on when he'd started drinking. Lady Bascomb would always invite him though because he was her cousin.

"Thank you, my lord. Edward!" She hurried toward her wayward guest just in time to save a pretty pink vase holding a huge arrangement of roses from crashing to the floor when Fenwick bumped into the table on which they sat.

Family could be such a trial.

Dismissing Lady Bascomb, Lord Fenwick, and the responsibilities of family duty, Sandy was finally rewarded for his patience when the door opened to admit Miss Devereaux and Mrs. Grey. After the ladies gave their wraps to the footman posted there for that sole reason, Sandy paused a moment to appreciate Miss Devereaux's lovely form. Her pale blue gown, shot through with silver made him think of a star in the early night sky. When she moved she sparkled, the candlelight hitting the metallic threads and making them twinkle. He could simply stand here and gaze at her the whole evening and be content. But that was rude and he would have a much better time conversing with her instead.

Indeed, the young lady was already looking at him quizzically.

"Good evening, Mrs. Grey, Miss Devereaux. I am here to fetch Miss Devereaux to cards with my cousin, Lord Boxtd, and Lady Augusta Hardy. We have been specially requested." Not exactly the truth, but Sandy had been summoned and he wished to partner Miss Devereaux, so according to his way of thinking she had been requested as well.

"Good evening, my lord." Mrs. Grey's broad smile as she curtsied told him he'd have no problem whisking her daughter away. "I am certain dear Isabelle is eager to play cards this evening, aren't you my dear?"

Miss Devereaux's expression was somewhat less enthusiastic, still she curtsied and nodded in agreement. "That is why we are here, Mama. To play cards and…" she cut her gaze toward Sandy, "to hopefully win wagers." She turned to stare directly at Sandy. "Is that not right, my lord?"

"My very sentiments, Miss Devereaux." The lady seemed prickly tonight. He'd have to attempt to smooth her out during their game. He offered his arm, marveling once more how perfectly they fit together. Her head came up exactly to his shoulder, so if he faced her, her mouth would be in exactly the proper place for a kiss.

Sandy shook that notion out of his head. A daydream for another time and place. Instead, he led her briskly toward the Egyptian room, so named because all of Lord Bascomb's treasures from that country were housed in that one room. Rumor had it that Lady Bascomb had refused to have the "heathen" antiques distributed throughout the house, and so the two had settled on a single room to hold them all. As a result, the decorations overpowered the small chamber, the dark blue wall painted with gold-leaf trim making it almost tomb-like. That room usually sent a chill of foreboding down Sandy's back, making him wonder if something sinister had occurred there at some point in time.

Tonight, however, when he and Miss Devereaux entered, the

only thing sinister about the room was the petulant look on his cousin Julius's face matched by the defiant one on Lady Augusta's, who sat next to him at the square card table. Next to him, not across from him as partners were always positioned.

His cousin rose as soon as they entered the room, a sullen look on his face.

"Good evening, Julius, Lady Augusta." From the dagger-like glances that flew between the two Sandy could surmise it was to be anything but a good evening. "Miss Devereaux, may I introduce my cousin, Lord Boxtd? And Lady Augusta Hardy?"

"How do you do, my lord, my lady." Miss Devereaux curtsied, shot Sandy a dubious look, then continued. "I am told we are to make up a set for whist. I do love to play cards so this should be quite an entertaining evening." She glanced from one angry face to the other. "I see I am to partner Lord Boxtd." With seamless grace, Miss Devereaux smiled warmly at his cousin. "I hope you are a keen player, my lord. I've been told the wagering is fierce in your family."

Julius's brows arched in a question to Sandy, then deepened into a frown when he flashed a look at Lady Augusta. He then seemed to come to himself and sent a genuine smile to Miss Devereaux. "I see my cousin has been telling tales out of school, but you have heard correctly. I can assure you, we will play to win, no matter the wager."

At that, Miss Devereaux sat down across from him and Julius took his seat again. "Come on, cousin. *Tempus fugit.* We must make the most of it as we are able."

With a heavy sigh, Sandy took his place opposite Lady Augusta, whose face now held a self-satisfied smirk. How had his scheme to spend time as Miss Devereaux's partner gone so awry? "So we should, cousin." Sandy sat and picked up the deck of cards. "Whose deal?"

The play that proceeded was swift and terrible.

Sandy and Lady Augusta won every hand save one that Miss Devereaux took by a fluke. They then played a second set with the same partners—at Lady Augusta's insistence—and with the same results. By the time he took the final trick, Miss Devereaux had managed to win a single hand once more. Julius, to his chagrin, had lost every hand. And while the wagering had been lackluster on everyone's part save Lady Augusta's, Julius and Miss Devereaux had lost a significant amount to them. Sandy was too embarrassed to suggest a third game, beside the fact that Julius was glaring at him as though he'd like to throttle him.

Although his cousin had seemed in a black mood from the moment Sandy entered the Egyptian room, Julius had gotten increasingly silent and sullen as his losses began to mount. Sandy had the idea that the root of the problem was his partner. Julius had wanted to partner Lady Augusta badly. What's more, the lady knew this and had neatly circumvented his cousin's arrangements for the game. After this evening Sandy might take Jules aside and talk to him seriously about abandoning his bid for Lady Augusta. The lady seemed not only disinterested but downright hostile to the idea of Julius's suit. Perhaps it was time to cry enough.

"I believe we've managed to thrash our opponents thoroughly enough for one evening, Lord MacKay. No need to venture into a third round of play." Lady Augusta all but crowed as she sat back, raking her half of the winnings toward her.

"Very well played, Lady Augusta, Lord MacKay." Miss Devereaux's even tone and warm smile served as rebuke enough to him and his partner in its sincere congratulations. "I fear whist was not my game tonight." She turned a consoling gaze on her partner. "I beg you to forgive me, Lord Boxtd. I seem to have done you no good at all this evening."

The storm clouds brewing in Julius's face, directed solely at Lady August, dissipated when he turned his gaze on his partner. "On the contrary, Miss Devereaux, it is I who must beg your pardon. I am the one who lost most abysmally. You tried to rally us by winning a hand here and there. I truly wish you'd had a better partner." He shot a look of pure misery at Lady Augusta.

"Would either of you ladies like a refreshment? I think I must change my location if I am to change my luck."

Neither lady accepted his offer, which made matters worse, and Julius took himself off with an offended huff.

"Well, I wish you would tell me, Sandy, what has gotten into your cousin. I've never seen him so surly." Lady Augusta sounded sincere, but a flicker of a smile gave her away.

"I'm sorry, Lady Augusta, but I'm afraid I haven't a clue. I haven't seen him act like this before." Of course he knew well and good what was eating at Jules. However, he couldn't very well speak of it and remain true to his cousin. He could, however, give the lady a hint if she needed one. He shrugged. "Perhaps he's in love. Men often act irrationally when Cupid's arrow skewers their hearts."

He took the cards and began to shuffle them. "Shall we play again? You will need to seek another partner, as I will claim Miss Devereaux for this next game."

Lady Augusta gave him a keen look, then shook her head. "I must go to my mother. I believe she had engaged me to Lord Pike for a set." She rose and Sandy jumped to his feet. "Good evening, my lord. Miss Devereaux. I wish you *bon chance* for the rest of the evening." The lady straightened her shoulders and left without a backward glance.

Sandy resumed his seat and breathed a sigh of relief. At last he had Miss Devereaux to himself. "I'm sorry we seem to be down a pair of partners." He continued to shuffle the deck, trying to think of a game that required only two players. Whatever happened, he did not intend to squander this opportunity. A novel idea reared its head. Why not take a totally different tack from his youngest cousin Tom? "Would you like to learn to play poker, Miss Devereaux?"

As soon as Lady Augusta left, Isabelle shook out her fan and commenced fanning herself vigorously. If she didn't cool down she thought she might catch fire. The room was warm, granted, however the heat that overpowered her currently stemmed from her emotional turmoil brought about during the whist game they had just finished. Had the problem been her poor performance at cards, she doubted she'd be so distraught, so that now alone with Lord MacKay she would revert back to her normal feelings. But no, she was still distressed and she didn't know why. Didn't want to admit why was closer to the truth.

"Would you like to learn to play poker, Miss Devereaux?" Lord MacKay sat nonchalantly shuffling the deck, for all the world as though he had not a care to his name. But his gaze rested on her, and that made all the difference.

Another time she'd love to lean a new card game with him, but she could scarcely keep her mind on the conversation at the moment. Trying to actually learn something would end up disastrously, with Lord MacKay thinking her the worst of ninnies and never wishing to call upon her again. He must think her the most abominable partner imaginable, given her recent performance with his cousin. Best not add more fuel to the fire. "As you can see, my lord, tonight is simply not my night for cards. I'd better leave it to another night, if you wouldn't mind. You saw my poor showing at whist—and I've been playing that game for years."

"Sometimes the cards simply don't fall your way, I'll admit that." He shuffled the cards one more time, then neatly dropped them into the ivory inlaid card box. "So if you will not play cards, how shall we pass the time?"

There might have been the faintest touch of suggestion in Lord MacKay's voice, but Isabelle actually welcomed it. She'd spent most of the games tense as a toad, wondering if Lady Augusta had set her cap for Lord MacKay. The lady obviously was disinterested in Lord Boxtd—painfully so as the evening progressed. Did that mean she'd requested Lord MacKay particularly to partner her and Lord MacKay had brought Isabelle along as a consolation prize for his cousin? Isabelle had been surprised she hadn't been partnered with Lord MacKay after his declaration yesterday, but tried to think nothing of it. Unfortunately, she could think of nothing else during their play. She'd been much more intent on Lord MacKay than her own partner, which had likely contributed to their overwhelming defeat. Every time Lord MacKay had met his partner's eyes, or smiled at her, or laughed, Isabelle had felt the stirrings of jealousy ignite in her soul.

Lord Boxtd also seemed to mark the couple, keeping his attention on Lady Augusta during most of the games. No wonder they had done so poorly at whist. Too distracted to form a strategy, Isabelle had discarded willy-nilly, which cost them hand after hand. Her partner had done no better, and she could sympathize with him wholeheartedly. Which, when she thought about it, made no sense whatsoever. Why should she be jealous of Lord MacKay paying attention to Lady Augusta? She certainly didn't wish to marry the gentleman.

But she had, somehow, come to expect Lord MacKay's attention to be focused solely on her. A foolish notion, to be sure. They'd scarcely met one another. It had been only two days since Lady Winslow's ball. And she'd long decided she couldn't entertain the idea of marriage at all.

Yet, now she apparently longed for Lord MacKay's attentions and resented anyone else who usurped them from her.

"Miss Devereaux?"

Isabelle shook her head, as if awakening from a dream. "Pardon me, my lord. I was—"

"Woolgathering?" His tone was rueful, but his eyes glinted with amusement. "By now you must have gathered together the largest bag of wool in London."

Laughing, Isabelle caught his eye and the warmest connection she'd ever experienced with another person made her glow with happiness. "I should become a sheep farmer, shouldn't I, my lord? I'd have an endless supply."

"No one would ever be able to gain your attention, Miss Devereaux. You'd be forever sheering and gathering the wool." His chuckle was deep and throaty, sending tingles down her spine. "I have sheep on my farms up in Scotland. You could gather wool there if you ever visit my castle in Carnwath."

Isabelle's breath caught in her throat, suddenly unsure of everything again. Was he or was he not attracted to her? That statement could be considered an invitation to visit him. Or she was making too much out of nothing. Probably the latter. Best to keep their banter light "Only after I've managed to purloin all the wool in England."

"At your given rate of woolgathering, that should be about," Lord MacKay took out a pocket watch and consulted it, "two hours and fifteen minutes from now."

Giggling at the nonsense they'd created together, Isabelle's tension relaxed. Lord, it was good to laugh again. To share such silliness. She'd been so sad and bitter for so long. Lord MacKay seemed to be able, as no one else had, to bring her out of herself. To make her forget…at least for a little while. Quite like an angel looking out for her, one might say.

"Well, if we cannot play cards," he punctuated that statement by shutting the card box, "and you are all out of wool to gather at the moment," his smile threatened to turn into laughter, "how can we best pass the time until you are whisked away to another table, Miss Devereaux?"

"The only thing two people who have nothing else to occupy themselves with usually do, my lord." To her surprise she blushed in a scandalously flirtatious manner.

He stared into her eyes and leaned toward her. "And what is that, Miss Devereaux?"

Swaying even closer to him she said, "Go to get refreshments, of course, my lord."

Lord MacKay stared deeply into her eyes for one moment more, then sat back, a rueful pucker to his lips. "I suppose woolgathering is thirsty work at that, Miss Devereaux."

Isabelle burst out laughing, great whoops that shook her to the bone. When finally she had quieted, she looked up at Lord MacKay who had risen and stood looking down at her, a suddenly tender look on his face as he offered his arm. "Will you please allow me to escort you to the refreshment room, Miss Devereaux."

Sober now, Isabelle nodded and eagerly slid her arm through his. He was warm and strong and comforting. He made her suddenly hope…for things she'd given up on long ago. Gazing up into his handsome, rugged face, Isabelle couldn't help but believe that this man was different from the others. That with him, some things might be possible.

Was she ready to take the next steps in her life? Ready to enjoy happiness for the first time in years? To accept that she deserved happiness in her life? Perhaps with Lord MacKay. Smiling into his face, she answered with joy in her voice. "Yes, my lord. I would like that very much." With a newfound boldness, she grinned. "You must keep your eye on me throughout the festivities to ensure I gather no more wool here at Lady Bascomb's."

"That I can promise to do, Miss Devereaux." His warm tone set her on fire anew, assuring that she would keep an eye on him all evening as well.

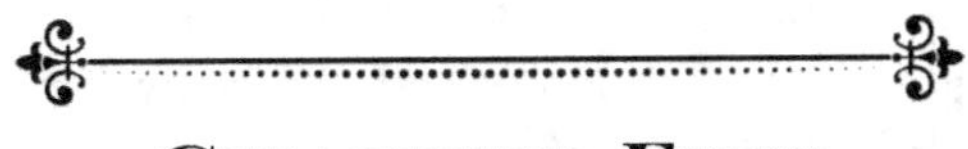

CHAPTER FIVE

September 22

"SHALL I FIX your hair in a new style this evening, miss?" Isabelle's lady's maid held the heated curling tongs in one expert hand, a slip of brown paper in the other.

"Yes, I think that would be lovely, thank you, Cooper." Isabelle turned her head from side to side, her fiery opal earrings bouncing and swaying with each movement. "I do want Lord MacKay to see me in a fresh look this evening." She'd become rather well versed in how to get and keep a gentleman's attention fixed upon her in the past fortnight. Well, she'd managed to keep Lord MacKay's attention on her, at least. That was all that really counted.

Over the past two weeks of parties and social entertainments, Isabelle had met with his lordship almost every night. They'd also driven out in his carriage most afternoons and he'd dined with her and Mama several times as well. All that time spent together had gone far toward persuading Isabelle that, should the gentleman actually make an offer for her hand, her answer would be a resounding yes. It was a far cry from their first meeting not quite a month ago, back when Isabelle couldn't wait to get away from him. Times had changed and so had she.

Now her feelings had altered so drastically, Isabelle couldn't fathom a day when she didn't meet Sandy. Of course, they hadn't exchanged first names yet. Isabelle had wanted to, had already begun to think of him by the informal name his friends and family used. But she hadn't quite gotten up the courage to ask him to call her Isabelle, although she was certain he'd be happy to do so. Perhaps tonight, she would move their friendship into a more intimate level by offering him her first name.

The thought of her name spoken in his deep, mellow voice—she could almost hear it, as though he had whispered it in her ear—made her twitch, impatient.

"Watch miss!" Cooper put a restraining hand on her shoulder. "You don't want me to be burning the hair off your head, do you?"

Isabelle froze. "Goodness, no. Thank you, Cooper. I will remain still as a stone." Her gaze tracked the tongs as Cooper expertly unwound them, leaving a long sausage curl dangling over her shoulder.

"That's better. You couldn't leave the house for a month with a whole clump of hair missing. I've heard of it happening." Cooper put hairpins in her mouth and began to coil the rest of Isabelle's hair into a chignon at the nape of her neck. "If the tongs are too hot, or a lady moves too suddenly, there could be a handful of hair burned off, and nothing to be done about it." Cooper took up the tongs again, once more heated sufficiently, then proceeded to roll the last of the hair on the other side of Isabelle's head. It had taken a long time for Isabelle to become used to the sizzle in her ear and the smell of burning hair in her nose.

"It's good to see you come out of yourself when Lord MacKay's around, miss. I'd say his attentions have been beneficial."

"I think so too, Cooper." Isabelle's gaze fell on her deep pink evening gown, with its lower cut bodice and puffy sleeves that showed off all her neck and shoulders. Festooned with delicate white lace on the edges and silk flowers of pink and blue at her waist, the gown boasted several layers of fabric, giving the ensemble a sophisticated air. This particular gown had been bespoken two weeks before, just after the card party at Lady Bascomb's. Subsequent to that evening of revelations, she had persuaded her mother she needed several new gowns if she was to hold Lord MacKay's interest. Mama had been only too happy to oblige her, and the result was this pink confection, the first to arrive from the seamstress, and just in time for tonight's ball.

She'd already promised Sandy three dances, the most she dared without censure from the *ton*. If they became formally betrothed, then she could dance every single dance with him—and would do so most willingly. Until then, she had to act with more decorum. She hoped with all her heart that the first dance would be a waltz. Whenever Sandy held her tightly, as in that intimate dance, Isabelle could scarcely keep herself from swooning. Oh, yes, her vinaigrette. She slipped the little vial into her reticule. Best be safe rather than sorry. She returned to her fanciful daydream about Sandy.

This time she imagined him holding her tightly, like in the waltz, but not in a waltz. In an embrace that ended, in her most secret imaginings, with him kissing her long and thoroughly. She shivered just thinking of it. All the conflicted feelings she'd felt for him melted away, became muted somehow, overcome by Sandy's good nature and kind attentions toward her. He was so agreeable, in fact, she'd come to think of him as her guardian angel, complete with halo. She trusted him as she trusted no other man on earth. It was quite a freeing feeling after years of suspicion and despair.

"There you go, miss. Take a look."

Isabelle gazed into the mirror on her toilette table and gasped. The new coiffure made her look much older, more mature and sophisticated, with an air of confidence she had hoped to exude for Sandy's benefit. Lord MacKay. She mustn't slip up and call him Sandy yet. "It's perfect, Cooper. Thank you."

"You've been more of a challenge recently, miss. And I must tell you, I've enjoyed it. I like to see you turned out well. You're a credit to your mother and your family." Cooper beamed at her as though she also took pride in Isabelle.

"You have plenty to be proud of yourself, Cooper. No one else would have badgered me so diligently to look my best when I didn't wish to go out in Society in the first place. What is it, Lucy?" The downstairs maid had knocked hurriedly, then opened the door before Isabelle could bid her do so.

"Oh, Miss Devereaux. You must come downstairs quickly." The girl's cheeks were pink with excitement. "You can't ever imagine what's happened, or who's downstairs with your mother!"

Isabelle put a hand up to her hair. Actually, she could imagine who was down there. Lord MacKay must have come to escort them to the ball as a surprise. "Tell Mama I'll be down directly, Lucy."

"Yes, miss." The girl bobbed a curtsy and ran out the door.

"I think the gold combs will complement the gown better than the silver, don't you, Cooper?"

"I do, miss." The maid inserted two delicate gold combs into the coil of hair and gave them a firm pat. "Now you'd best go down." Cooper's gaze met Isabelle's in the mirror. "You think it's Lord MacKay waiting, don't you miss?"

Unable to stop herself, Isabelle smiled broadly. "I do, Cooper. He must be eager to see me if he's come to escort us without prior arrangement." Isabelle's heart beat faster just supposing what that might mean. She rose, checked in the mirror again, and bit her lips to deepen the color. Truly she looked her best tonight. What a fortuitous thing that her gown arrived just in time. After one last glance in the looking glass, she turned for the door.

"Don't forget your shawl, Miss Devereaux." Cooper draped a lacy pink and white China silk shawl over her shoulders.

Isabelle gathered her reticule, made sure her fan and vinaigrette were in it, then tied the little bag to her wrist. "Let us hurry, Cooper. I don't want to keep Lord MacKay waiting."

They descended the stairs swiftly, Isabelle's excitement growing with each footfall. Tonight would certainly be the night she asked him to use her first name. That thought brought a smile to her lips while heat touched her cheeks, though there was nothing to be embarrassed about surely.

She reached the first floor, Cooper right behind her, then slowed when an odd, unexpected sound reached her. Cocking her head, Isabelle approached the front parlor with mounting trepidation.

Someone was sobbing.

Isabelle glanced back at Cooper, whose brows had pinched together. So, her maid had heard it also. Isabelle stopped just outside the door, trying to understand why her mother—for it was unmistakably now her mother—was weeping. The sobbing was punctuated at intervals by low mutterings Isabelle could not understand.

Completely unnerved now, Isabelle gave Cooper another fearful glance, but there seemed nothing for it but to enter to discover what was the matter. Lifting her head and straightening her shoulders, Isabelle entered the parlor and stopped dead upon seeing her mother in the arms of a gentleman who was assuredly not Lord MacKay.

This gentleman, to whom Mama was clinging like the Rock of Gibraltar, stood almost a foot taller than Lord MacKay. His head was bent, hidden by her mother's, so she couldn't see his face. He appeared to be a burly gentleman as well as tall. Attired in a dark grey pea coat, he must be a naval officer of some sort. Perhaps a merchant friend of her stepfather's. But what was he doing here, at this time of night, with her mother crying in his arms.

"Mama? Whatever is the matter?"

Startled, her mother jumped away from the man, and wiped tears from her eyes as her mouth tried to pull upward in a smile. "Oh, Isabelle!" She glanced up into the man's face and the smile jerked wider. "It's a miracle, my dear."

"What miracle, Mama?" Her mother's words and countenance made no sense.

"I am the miracle, Isabelle." The gentleman straightened and turned toward her.

Isabelle's legs turned to water. Her heart gave a great surge and for a moment, the world around her turned gray. Clutching her chest, she stumbled backward into Cooper, who caught her, but Isabelle continued to back away. It couldn't be true. Her heart now sped up, beating so fast she couldn't catch her breath. He couldn't be here. *He was dead.*

"I've come home, daughter." The ghost of Ambrose Grey, her stepfather lost at sea over three years ago, smiled at her.

Her legs buckled.

The tall figure came toward her as she slumped to the floor and the world went gray—then blessedly black.

WITH A GASP, Isabelle sat up, the awful acrid smell of *sal volatile* in her nose. Cooper stoppered the vinaigrette and slipped it back into her reticule. "Are you better now, miss?"

"What happened?" Isabelle's head was spinning, the sharp smell of ammonia seemingly clinging to her nose. Stomach roiling, she hoped she wouldn't shoot the cat all over her new gown.

"I'm so sorry, my dear."

The voice. Dear Lord, it *was* his voice. The memory of seeing Ambrose Grey just now, apparently back from the dead, surfaced in her mind.

"After seeing me alive and well, you were overcome, my dear." Her stepfather came around the chaise they had laid her on. "I am truly sorry to have startled you so badly."

Slowly, Isabelle lifted her gaze to his face, the blandly pleasant features, slightly protruding eyes, and snub nose she remembered too well. Now, however, his face seemed more gaunt, older, the fine lines around his eyes deeper. But it was the same face nonetheless.

This must be a nightmare. She prayed it was a horrible apparition brought on by who knew what trick of the mind. But she could feel the cushions of the chaise beneath her, smell the lingering odor of the smelling salts, and sense Cooper's steadying hand on her shoulder, thank God. Very well. Despite what she'd believed true and privately rejoiced over, Ambrose Grey had returned from the dead. So what in God's name was she going to do now?

"Isabelle." Her mother's strained voice gave truth to the horrendous reality. "Can you believe it, my dear?" Mama took Ambrose's arm. "Lucy told me a gentleman had come and of course, I thought it was Lord MacKay. I told her to put him in the parlor thinking he was here to escort us to the ball."

Exactly as Isabelle herself had thought.

"Can you imagine my shock—well, yes, I suppose you can, dearest—when I entered the room to find Ambrose, alive and well after we'd thought he'd drowned so many years ago." Mama's eyes were bright with tears. "I still cannot take it in, my dear." She led him to the largest of the parlor's chairs and urged him to sit, then lowered herself onto the sofa, as though her legs might give out too. "But Ambrose, please tell us how you come to be here."

Her stepfather cut his eyes at Mama, then nodded. "It is quite a tale, my dear."

Drawing a deep breath to steady herself, Isabelle eased her legs over the side of the chaise until she was sitting more or less on her own. Cooper's hand still rested on her shoulder, a blessing of strength.

Stretching out his long legs, Ambrose settled back in the chair. His gaze flicked from her mother to her, making certain their attention was completely focused on him, then began. "In May of 1857, I put out to sea from Kingston on my return trip to London with a cargo of molasses for Samuels & Sons. The journey was quite uneventful until the *Cordelia* ran into a storm off the coast of the Canary Islands."

This information had come to Isabelle and her mother late in June, once the *Cordelia* had been overdue for weeks.

"She foundered on a rocky shoal, broke apart, then went down in minutes. I stayed aboard as long as I could, but in the end was thrown into the water and had to watch the ghastly scene as I clung to a cask of the molasses that had broken out of the hold. Perhaps half the crew survived the wreck, but we floated apart in the next few days. Eventually, I fetched up on one of the smaller islands to the west of the Canaries. I'm not sure it even has a name. I washed up on shore barely alive after days at sea without food or water, simply glad to be alive."

Isabelle sighed. He might so easily have *not* survived. Such a wicked thought, but not an ounce of remorse did she have for thinking it.

"The island was uninhabited, but lush with vegetation. I managed to survive on fish and crab and molasses, plus some other small game I caught for what turned out to be almost three years." Ambrose sighed and patted her mother's hand. "I began to believe I'd be marooned on that God-forsaken rock forever, until about three months ago, a French ship, the *Saint Michel,* also wrecked on my island." Ambrose chuckled. "You can imagine how amazed they were to find me there."

"They must have been shocked, my dear." Mama rushed to agree with him. She must remember how he liked to see her be attentive to his tales.

"Fortunately, their ship's damage could be repaired. I offered my assistance in exchange for transportation back to France. They put me off in Marseille and after a month or so, I managed to secure passage on an English frigate, the *Apollonia*. She put in last week at Dover." He smiled and spread his hands wide. "So here I am."

"Why didn't you write to us from Marseille, Ambrose?" Mama's voice pretended to scold him, but in a teasing way she used to use that didn't make him angry. "I would have wanted to know you were alive and on your way back to us."

Isabelle's stepfather sighed. "I would have done that, Miranda, but I had lost faith. I was afraid that you had remarried, my love." He peered at her, searching her eyes for some hidden truth about her faithfulness to him. "I wanted to come to London, get word of you, see for myself that you had not come to care for another." Ambrose stroked her mother's cheek and Isabelle closed her eyes against the image. "I wanted to see how it was with you and Isabelle before I made myself known to you."

"What if Mama had remarried, Ambrose?" Isabelle forced herself to look at him. "What would you have done then?"

"I'm not quite sure, my dear." His gaze bore into her. "Thankfully, that trial has been spared us."

Isabelle stared down at her hands lying rigid in her lap. The moment she'd begun to hope for happiness once more, that hope had been dashed as surely as her stepfather's ship had been in the dreadful waves of the Atlantic.

"Isabelle."

Willing herself not to flinch, she raised her gaze to him.

"You have become a most beautiful woman while I was away." He took in her form from bottom to top, his gaze coming to rest just below her face. "I am very sorry to have missed those years when you blossomed into a young lady. I couldn't be more proud of you if you were my own daughter."

But she wasn't, thank God for his tender mercies. She ought to say something in return. It would be unnatural not to, but for the life of her, she couldn't summon a single word. Let them think her still stunned by his appearance. That wasn't far from the truth anyway.

"You're dressed for a ball this evening, your mother said. I am certain you are a most popular partner with all the gentlemen." Ambrose stared straight into her face, making her shiver.

"She is the particular favorite of Lord MacKay, Ambrose. A more charming gentleman does not exist, saving yourself, my dear." Mama's smile couldn't get any wider unless her mouth split. "I fear he will be terribly disappointed not to be able to partner dear Isabelle this evening. However, he will understand completely once he's told of the miracle that prevented our attendance at the ball tonight."

"No!" Isabelle bounded to her feet. "I refuse to disappoint Lord MacKay this evening, Mama. I think it most imprudent."

"But my dear." Mama's face looked suddenly frightened. "We cannot go out. Ambrose will be too tired to accompany us and we cannot leave him alone when he's just come back to us. It is the only proper thing to do. Lord MacKay—"

"Lord MacKay is on the verge of a declaration for my hand in marriage, Ambrose." Isabelle shot a defiant look at him, the first time tonight she'd been able to look him in the face willingly. "I want to do nothing that would deter him from asking me to marry him." A moment of inspiration hit. "Why don't you and Mama remain here and celebrate your return. Meanwhile, I will attend the ball with Cooper as my chaperone." That was scarcely ever done, but this was a desperate situation. She must see Sandy—Lord MacKay, that was—without fail this evening.

"But Isabelle, that simply isn't done." Her mother's face bore the sternest lines Isabelle had ever seen. "You will stay with us and welcome your father home."

On the tip of her tongue to shout "He's not my father!," Isabelle was saved from exacerbating the conflict by Ambrose's firm voice.

"Miranda, we should not interfere with Isabelle's plans for the evening, especially if she's on the brink of receiving a proposal." His eyes drifted from her mother's face to hers, a thoughtful light in them. "I, for one, would like to meet this gentleman who aspires to my daughter's hand." His eyes narrowed and Isabelle braced herself. "I think we should all go to the ball. Then Isabelle can save a dance for me as well."

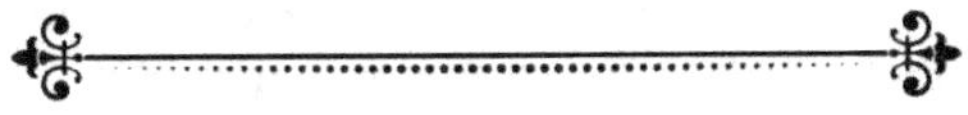

Chapter Six

When Isabelle, her mother, and Ambrose entered Mrs. Hatch's townhouse, Isabelle wasn't at all prepared for the onslaught of people eager to speak to and congratulate her stepfather on his miraculous return. *En masse,* the *ton* descended upon them the moment they walked through the door. Mrs. Hatch looked flabbergasted, as though she'd been given an unexpected and exclusive gift. Of course, the papers would be full of the news tomorrow morning, so in essence, she'd stolen a march on every other hostess, all of whom would want Captain Grey at their entertainments throughout the rest of the Little Season.

The inundation actually saved Isabelle. Her mother and Ambrose were so busy greeting all their admirers, Isabelle was able to slip away from them undetected. She drifted over to an open space beside the orchestra, took a moment to breathe, then scanned the ballroom, searching not for Sandy, but for her bosom friend, Grace Horton. After a moment, she spied Grace, standing just outside the spreading circle of people surrounding Isabelle's mother. She hurried toward her friend, placing a hand on her arm. "Grace."

"Isabelle!" Her friend squealed and hugged her fiercely. "My goodness, just think of the news. Everyone is talking about the nine days wonder of Captain Grey's miraculous return." Her friend's eyes, always a bright blue, were now sparkling with excitement. "Isn't it wonderful? Aren't you thrilled to pieces?"

More than anything Isabelle wanted to shout, "No!" To tell someone how horrible this news was for her. But she forced herself to refrain from an outburst that she couldn't afford, not if she wanted a life with Sandy. "It is wonderful, isn't it? And such a surprise." She stared at the throng chatting away with Mama and her husband. "We just found out ourselves before we came here. I cannot imagine how everyone else knows."

"Oh, I can tell you that." Grace eagerly drew closer. "My mother had it from Lady Dasher who had it from Lord Dasher that Captain Grey went to his club—which is Lord Dasher's club as well—directly after the captain reached London. He said he wished to attend to his toilette, including a haircut and shave before he went home. Otherwise, your mother might not have let him in."

That was too much to have hoped for.

Leaning closer, Grace whispered, "Do you think his hair and beard were long and wild-looking, Isabelle? They say he had to borrow a set of clothing because he had none save hand-me-downs from someone on the ship that rescued him."

"I would think, with having several weeks from the moment he put into port in France, he would have had time for his ablutions and could have availed himself of a barber's services before now." It seemed as though her stepfather wished to be given credit for taking the forethought to arrange his haircut and clothing before he went to see his family, even though, according to him, he had several weeks to do this very thing.

"Perhaps he was so overwhelmed by being rescued, he didn't think to do it until later."

Sighing, Isabelle supposed everyone would want to give Ambrose the benefit of the doubt about everything now. With a look to the slowly thinning crowd around Ambrose, Isabelle nodded. "It seems as though all the members of his club spread the word of his arrival with the speed of Pegasus."

"Do you blame them, Isabelle? This is the most glorious thing to happen in an age." Her friend turned to her with starry eyes. "What did you do when you first saw him?"

"I fainted."

"Gracious, Isabelle!" Grace squealed, drawing the attention of several matrons waiting to speak to Ambrose. They made note of the two girls, then put their heads back together.

"I thought he was a ghost." If not for all this hullabaloo, she still might have a hope that was true.

"As well you might." Grace shook her head, staring toward Isabelle's stepfather. "I might have done the same thing." She shivered. "I might have screamed."

Isabelle had wanted to scream all evening but had managed to restrain herself so far. The struggle continued. "It was enough to frighten anyone." She must get to her reason for seeking out Grace. "But I sought you out just now to ask if I might stay with you for several days."

The astonishment on Grace's face almost made Isabelle laugh. Regrettably, it was no laughing matter."

"Why would you wish to do that when your father has just returned practically from the dead?"

"My stepfather." Isabelle had to curb her desire to snap at Grace. "I thought it would be more considerate for me to be out from underfoot while he and my mother were getting reacquainted."

Eyes big, Grace's cheeks went cherry red. "Oh, of course they would wish…to be together…after such a long time apart."

"Exactly." Thank goodness she didn't have to explain it in more embarrassing detail to her friend. She hated to abandon her mother, but he was her husband, after all. "I would only be in the way and then, of course, I'd be going out each evening, dragging them to entertainments, like tonight, when I'm certain they would much rather remain at home alone."

"That does make sense, Isabelle." Her friend's cheeks had returned to a normal color, her mouth again in a smile. "Let me go ask mother, but I'm certain it will be fine, especially when I explain why you wish to come. Mother is so sensitive to such things." She started to go, then halted, thinking. "You can come for luncheon tomorrow and stay through the weekend or even until next week. It will be nice to have someone to be with as we prepare to go out. It's been lonely since my sister married." Grace's gaze darted around the room until she spied her mother in the thick of the hub of people surrounding Isabelle's parents. "There she is." She waggled her fingers as she left. "I'll see you after the first set."

Relief washed through Isabelle, making her shoulders slump. She'd hoped against hope for such a swift invitation. Grace had been a true friend always. One of the few people Isabelle could count on, even if she couldn't quite confide in her completely. But visiting her friend's home would take care of almost a week during which she could figure something out. Perhaps a hasty trip to visit her grandmother in Northern England could be arranged.

Unfortunately, that still left tonight to worry about, both here and later at home. To deter her stepfather once they returned home, she'd consult Cooper first chance she got and arrange for the maid to stay in Isabelle's bed tonight. Hopefully that would keep her stepfather's violence at bay. Even if he threatened to sack Cooper to get her out of the room, Isabelle could assure her she'd not lose her position if she remained steadfast. Perhaps if she'd had a lady's maid three years ago, it would have made a difference. But she'd been young and expected to tend to her own needs while in the schoolroom.

That left the time spent here at the ball to be worked out, but if she could enlist Sandy's aid, all should be well. He seemed a very resourceful gentleman. She must go in search of him this instant. Pulling out her dance card, a quiver of trepidation shot through her. Although her first dance had been promised to Sandy, most of the other spaces were blank. She could not allow them to remain so. Her stepfather would make good on his chilling words as they left the house.

At that moment, the strains of the orchestra tuning up sounded throughout the ballroom. Isabelle sighed with relief and immediately scanned the crowd for her partner. There he was. Relief was tempered with annoyance for he had emerged from the horde still gathered around her mother and stepfather. Reluctant to go even that close to them, she continued to stand and stare at Sandy, willing him to look her way.

At last he spied her, his face lighting up as he did, then hurried toward her.

As he approached, fear suddenly shot through Isabelle. Was Sandy truly the man she believed him to be? Would he understand the horror she'd gone through? More importantly, would he agree to help protect her?

"Miss Devereaux, what an extraordinary evening it must be for you." Sandy bowed, smiling broadly. "I spoke with your mother and stepfather just now. It is amazing that such luck came your way."

Stomach churning, Isabelle feared she'd be terribly ill if Sandy didn't stop prattling on about her good luck. Everyone's starry-eyed gushing over Ambrose Grey was about to make her retch in public. She had to make Sandy stop so she grabbed his hand. "They are starting the dance now." Without another word, she towed him onto the ballroom floor. It wasn't the most elegant action, but it worked. Sandy stood beside her, mouth agape. "Well, we needed to take our places."

The orchestra struck up the tune—a polka, thank goodness—and they were off in the exuberant dance.

"You seem ill-at-ease this evening, Miss Devereaux. Sandy held her tightly at the waist, usually evoking a sense of joy in her.

Tonight, it was torture.

"I am sorry." Isabelle fought to smile brightly. "It has been an exceptional day."

"I cannot imagine." His brow furrowed. "I find I am surprised you are here at all. I'd have thought you'd remain at home in a private celebration."

Isabelle had to grit her teeth and concentrate on the steps of the polka before she could form an answer that wouldn't reveal her true feelings. "Mama and Ambrose very kindly did not wish for me to lose the opportunity of dancing this evening." She stared meaningfully into his eyes. "I did not wish to give up the chance to dance with you."

Sandy cocked his head. "You call your stepfather by his given name? Not Father?"

"No, not since I was a child." Not precisely the truth, but close enough. "I think also they wish to share their happiness with the *ton*." She nodded to the thinning throng and caught Ambrose staring at her.

A dark, assessing stare.

Isabelle gasped and squeezed Sandy's hand. Oh, this was what she'd feared. Another glance back at her stepfather caught him nodding to her mother, then starting for the dance floor just as the music ended.

"Take me outside, quickly," she whispered in his ear. "We mustn't let anyone see us." The desperation in her voice obviously galvanized him to act without thought.

He swung her around and headed for a group of laughing couples, just quitting the dance floor. They wove between them, then sped around the room to the first set of doors leading to the verandah. He checked over his shoulder, was satisfied they weren't watched, then slipped outside.

The cool autumn air made Isabelle shiver, but its crispness allowed her to draw a deep breath for the first time since the reappearance of her stepfather. Her head cleared and she pulled the dance card from her wrist and thrust it into Sandy's hands. "For the love of God, fill this completely with your name, Sandy."

STARTLED TO HIS soul by her use of his first name—the nickname of his first name at that—Sandy could only gape at Miss Devereaux while his mind tried to sort out her scandalous request. To fill a young lady's dance card with one gentleman's name alone was unheard of. No young lady gave all her dances to a single man unless they were affianced. And much as he might like to think it, he didn't believe Miss Devereaux intended to use this unorthodox method to propose to him. What he did know was that she had been distraught the entire time they had been together this evening. Now he had to find out why.

The resurrection of her stepfather could be to blame, however his miraculous appearance should have made the lady distracted in a good way. When in doubt, best be direct. "Miss Devereaux, can you please tell me what is the matter?" After several moments, when she only stood there looking miserable, he decided drastic measures must be taken. "Isabelle, please. You can tell me what is wrong. You must know I will help you in any way I can."

The use of her given name—which he'd been savoring in his mind for weeks now—must have struck a chord within her. She stared at him for a moment, almost as if coming to herself from far away, then burst into tears.

"Oh, God, Sandy. I don't know what to do." She panted as though she'd never catch her breath again. "I saw him looking at us…staring at me when we were dancing, and…when the dance was ending, he started toward us. And I knew…I just knew he was going to ask me to dance with him and I can't, Sandy. I cannot do it."

"Who, Isabelle?" This was madness. Who could she be so afraid of? "Who has frightened you so badly?"

"Ambrose." The word was barely a whisper. "My stepfather."

"Captain Grey?" Sandy stumbled back a step. That was the last name he'd expected to hear. "You're afraid of your stepfather?"

"Yes, oh Sandy, yes." She flung herself at him, wrapping her arms around him in an abandonment he'd never believed of her.

Trembling like a leaf in a high wind, she clung to him. Her tears soaked the breast of his jacket, making a dark spot on the wool. Not that he cared a fig. Gingerly, he lifted her away. He needed to see her face. "What did he do?"

The misery in her face was pitiful to see and sent a sinking feeling to the pit of his stomach. Sobs shook her again and he pulled her back to him, cradling her. She could tell him when she was ready. Of course, if Captain Grey was searching for her, they didn't have much time at all. "Can you tell me, my dear?"

The endearment caught her off guard, as he'd hoped, and she drew back, her eyes shiny with tears. She took a deep breath and closed her eyes. "He…he hurt us. Both my mother and me." Her eyes flew open, her gaze darting around fearfully, as though she expected the man to materialize before her. "He'd done it for years. So much so, I'd become used to it. But before he left that last time, something came over him. He changed for the worse and I can't tell you why." She shrugged. "Perhaps money was the problem, but I really don't know. I was still in the schoolroom, but I'd overhear things. Arguments between him and my mother. Afterward, Mama would appear in tight, high-necked, long-sleeved gowns. Sometimes she'd have the shadow of a bruise on her cheek."

The longer Isabelle spoke, the tighter Sandy gripped her hands until he had to release them or break her bones. "You said he struck you as well?"

She hesitated so long, Sandy began to doubt she'd answer, but finally she nodded. "Before he sailed that last time, he beat us so badly, we couldn't go out for weeks afterward. Until long after he was gone." Isabelle hung her head. "I was so glad, so thankful when he was reported dead. I tried to feel some remorse, but I couldn't. I know that's wrong, but I couldn't help it. It was true. Now…" She stood staring at nothing, her face drained of all color by the pale moonlight, "I don't know what to do. I can't let him do that again, Sandy. I simply can't."

Staring at her distress, watching it mount by the moment, Sandy's first inclination was to call the man out and put a bullet through his black heart. Unfortunately, that wouldn't do at all if they wanted to avoid a scandal of epic proportions, even by *ton* standards. He supposed he could hire a bunch of miscreants to ambush the man and thrash him within an inch of his life. But of course, then the wretched man wouldn't know why he'd been set upon and so not know to desist with his foul treatment of Isabelle and her mother. It was a conundrum that could at least wait for a day or two, giving him time to ponder the form of retribution that would follow. The moment's pressing business was helping Isabelle stay out of the man's clutches on the ballroom floor. That dilemma Sandy could solve forthwith.

"Much as I would love to fill your dance card with no name but my own—" he tapped the little card against his other hand, "—I fear that would be too scandalous. Allow me, instead, to fill it for you. Can you allow me to escort you to the ladies' retiring area?"

Isabelle nodded, eyes downcast.

"Good." He lifted her face to his, transfixed once more by its beauty, even though its lines were etched with fear. "I'm afraid I have been quite cavalier in using your given name this evening, Miss Devereaux. You caught me off guard by using mine earlier."

"I must confess I've been using yours in my mind for some time, my lord." Isabelle's cheeks blushed faintly. "I would like very much to continue using it, if I may. And I invite you to use mine as well."

"That is a privilege I will be forever grateful to accept...Isabelle." He raised her hand and kissed it. "Now let me take you to the retiring room until I can manage your dance card."

Fortunately, the orchestra was in the middle of a spritely Scottish reel. Sandy led Isabelle behind the jumping dancers, all the way around the dance floor to the retiring room, a small receiving chamber behind the orchestra that had been set aside for that purpose. "Please stay inside until I return for you, my dear."

She shot him a look—half gratitude, half hope.

Through sheer dint of will, Sandy turned away. More than anything, he wanted to take her in his arms and assure her everything would be all right. Because it would be. He would see to that.

Clutching her little dance card in his hand, Sandy hurried over to a group of gentlemen laughing and talking to the side of the dance floor. By good fortune, one of their number was his cousin, Ulysses Quartermain.

"Sandy, well met." Yule slapped him on the back, his eyes lighting with sincere pleasure.

"Well met, cousin. Gentlemen." Sandy bowed to the crowd, all of whom he enjoyed a passing acquaintance with.

"We were just marveling over the return of Captain Grey." Yule's brows rose. "You're courting his daughter, aren't you?" His cousin's grin broadened. "Going to have to come up to scratch now that she's got a protective father to deal with, won't you, old chap?"

In that moment, when it was on the tip of his tongue to tell Yule what a monster the miracle man actually was, Sandy comprehended that he could never expose the truth about Miss Devereaux's dance card. At least, not now. The scandal would be every bit as heinous as if he called the man out. Better to make the reason less of desperation, more of a kindness.

"Indeed, Yule, I've got to mind my manners even more particularly now. It's quite the nine days wonder, don't you know?" He peered at the faces surrounding him. Four of the gentlemen he knew very well, plus Yule would do nicely. There were two gentlemen he knew but slightly. Still, he could make the introductions when necessary. Even standing up with a stranger would be preferable to dancing with her brute of a father. "I need to enlist your help, gentlemen. All of you."

His cousin's face changed from jovial to concerned. "What's the matter, cousin?"

The other men perked up at the summons, their complete attention on Sandy.

"Miss Devereaux, while elated at her father's return, is feeling somewhat left out of the celebration." Improvising wildly, he hit on the very thing to gain the men's cooperation. "They arrived late to the ball and her dance card is sadly empty because of it. I've given her three dances and would give her more if the *ton* allowed it. So, I decided I would fill her card for the night so that she's never without a partner. That way she will feel special for herself amidst all the fanfare for her father's return."

Before he'd even finished speaking, Yule reached for the all but blank card. "Of course, Sandy. I am free for several dances still. I will be happy to stand up with Miss Devereaux. Gentlemen…" He finished signing his name with a flourish, and held it out to the others in the circle. "Will you help make the lady feel appreciated this evening?"

His friends nodded and murmured in agreement. Then one by one they took the card and wrote their names again and again until there were no blank spaces left.

"My great thanks, gentlemen." Sandy took the card back, taking care the pencil markings didn't smear. "Miss Devereaux will be thrilled." He turned to go, then stopped and turned back. "If I may beg another boon of you, gentlemen. I'm sure you would all like to ask Miss Devereaux about the return of her father, but I beg you not to. We wish to make the lady believe you are interested in her, not her father."

A murmur of agreement went around the circle of gentlemen.

"Thank you." He bowed and looked to his cousin. "Yule, I will bring Miss Devereaux to you before the next dance begins as I believe that is your name there?"

"So it is, cousin. I await Miss Devereaux eagerly."

With a grateful nod, Sandy hurried away, back to the ladies' retiring room, calmer and more secure in the knowledge that his Isabelle was safe from the clutches of that monster.

His Isabelle. In his mind she was his. Now all he needed to do was make it so.

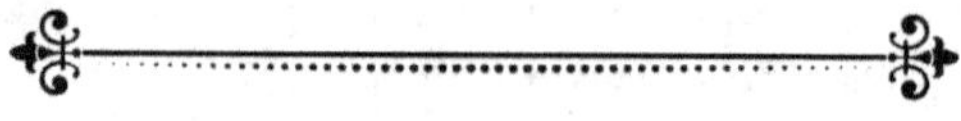

Chapter Seven

Briskly, Sandy approached the ladies' retiring room, Isabelle's full dance card in hand, then stopped, flummoxed. How was he to fetch her out of the room? He couldn't very well barge in, and there were no other ladies lurking about he might send in to get her. Shouting her name would only draw undue attention. Of course, he could knock…but oh, this was embarrassing.

Luckily for him, as he was raising a hand to the door, it opened and two young ladies, Lady Emily Lane and Lady Elizabeth Currie, came out. Sandy stumbled back a pace, then bowed, hoping his face hadn't gone red. "Lady Elizabeth, Lady Emily, good evening."

Both of them giggled, as only young ladies could, and curtsied. "Lord MacKay, good evening."

"I trust you are enjoying the ball?"

"Yes, my lord, very much." Lady Emily, the elder of the two cousins, batted her long dark eyelashes at him as she smiled broadly. "May we help you with anything, my lord?"

Blast it, this was not the time for a flirtation. He knew her brother, Lord Benington, well and he'd not take kindly to any such nonsense with his youngest sister. "Indeed you may, my lady. Did you happen to see Miss Devereaux in the retiring room?"

"Yes, my lord," Lady Elizabeth spoke up. "She's sitting just inside."

"Would you do me the favor of telling her I have returned to escort her to her next partner?"

"I'd be happy to do so, my lord." Lady Emily spoke up quickly. She opened the door, glanced back over her shoulder and gave him another flirtatious look. "Wait right there."

Sandy cringed inwardly. "Thank you."

Lady Emily disappeared into the retiring room and Sandy sighed in relief.

"Don't mind Emily, my lord." Lady Elizabeth shook her head. "She's determined to have as much fun as possible at every entertainment and therefore doesn't care what she says or does. Her mother has tried to curb her high spirits, but her methods do not seem to be working."

"She does seem in particularly good spirits tonight." Sandy's gaze dropped to Lady Elizabeth's hand, where her dance card dangled. "I believe I will add to them. May I repay your kindness by asking for a dance, my lady? If you have one left, that is."

The young lady beamed at him and held out her card. "I have just one left, my lord. It is as though it was waiting for you."

With a smile, Sandy added his name for the fourth dance and gave the card back.

"Thank you." She glanced at him, a slight smile on her lips. "I have done very little to deserve your kind request, my lord. I wonder how you plan to repay my cousin who actually assisted you?"

"With a similar request for a dance, my lady." Sandy grinned at her. "Will that not be enough?"

"Oh, I daresay she will make something more of a dance than you expect." Lady Elizabeth grinned back at him.

Sandy sighed. This night was turning into much more than he'd planned for. Still, one must pay one's debts, no matter the cost.

The ladies emerged from the retiring room at last, Isabelle

looking at him expectantly. She looked a bit calmer than before. Perhaps the short rest away from the crowds had done her good. "Thank you, Lady Emily."

"You are very welcome, my lord." The lady batted her eyes at him once more.

"May I ask if you…have a dance open, Lady Emily?" The question came out more halting than he would have liked, but he had done his duty.

"I do my lord." She bounded over to him, her card extended. "I have two, in fact."

Sandy grasped the pencil and scribbled his name in the slot for the fifth dance. "I will take this one, as I am engaged to Miss Devereaux for the other one."

"Very well, my lord." Giggles burst from Lady Emily once more as she grasped Lady Elizabeth's arm. "I will see you shortly."

The two cousins hurried away, their heads together, peals of their laughter lingering even after they had emerged into the ballroom.

"*Your* dance card now seems to be full, my lord." Isabelle gave him a keen look.

"A good thing, as otherwise I will have to stand by and watch as you dance in the arms of many different gentlemen this evening. Here you are, my dear." He handed her dance card over. "Filled to the brim with bachelors eager to dance with you all evening long."

Staring at the little card in his hand, Isabelle plucked it from his fingers as if mesmerized. "You really did it, Sandy?"

"I would do anything for you, Isabelle."

Her gaze met his, then her cheeks grew rosy pink and she looked away. "I suppose I should have asked if you wish me to call you Sandy. Or would you prefer Saunders?"

He shook his head and snorted. "Sandy, please. Saunders is what my mother called me when I was a bad little boy. It was often followed by several stinging smacks of a ruler to my backside, so by all means, Sandy is more preferable."

Isabelle laughed for the first time that evening, a joyously sweet sound that Sandy knew he'd want to hear in every room of his house for the rest of his life. Her smiling face was the one he wanted to kiss every day too. In this moment, he knew exactly what he wanted.

The area around the ladies' retiring room, however, was hardly the place for a declaration. Well, he could remedy that. He grasped her arm and pulled her to him. "Come with me. We haven't much time. Yule will be here any minute to claim his dance."

Wide-eyed, she nodded and followed him willingly back toward the ballroom. Before they reached it however, he pulled her into a small receiving room, deserted save for a friendly fire.

He carefully positioned them until they stood face to face, her head slightly cocked, brows furrowed over two brilliant sapphire eyes. Which immediately widened to enormous circles as Sandy went down on one knee.

"Miss Devereaux, although we have not known one another very long, I am absolutely certain that I wish to be the only gentleman in your life. The only one who will be allowed to cherish you, to love and protect you until eternity claims us both." He clasped her hand, the chill in it making him chafe it just a bit to warm it. "Isabelle, will you please make me the happiest of men and consent to be my wife?"

TEARS STREAMING DOWN her face, Isabelle trembled inside, unable to make herself believe this was really and truly happening. Until recently, she'd never even dreamed this would happen to her. Only after meeting Sandy, the kindest, most gentle of men had she dared to think she could trust a man after the horror she'd experienced with her stepfather. But Sandy was different. At least, she'd almost persuaded herself he was different. He still didn't know all of her story. Could she trust that he would understand when he did find out? That was the sole reason she now hesitated, when she yearned to accept him at once. Was she willing to risk everything in order to gain her heart's desire? Considering the alternative—continuing to live under the same roof as her stepfather—there simply was no other option. She must embrace this future—with its tempting chance for happiness—and pray Sandy was the man she believed him to be in her heart.

Nodding uncontrollably, it took Isabelle a moment to finally stutter out a heartfelt answer. "Yes."

The look of joy that spread over Sandy's face made her heart beat faster and her knees grow weak. Dare she hope that fondness she'd glimpsed in his eyes might turn into something deeper? She would gladly accept him as simply husband and friend, but if there was a hope she could aspire to gain his love…That was truly a dangerous mark for which to aim. Her own heart was already fully engaged, beyond reason given their relatively short acquaintance. To hope that love would be returned…was tempting and frightening all at once.

Smile broadening as he rose, Sandy grasped her shoulders and drew her close. "You have made me the happiest man alive, Isabelle. I will do everything within my power to love and cherish and protect you all the days of our lives."

He'd said it. Actually said the word. Love. He loved her. Warmth as she'd never known before engulfed Isabelle and tears fell down her cheeks once more. Tears of joy such as she'd never cried before. Her life henceforth could be more different than she'd ever believed it could.

Sandy pulled her closer still, put a finger under her chin, and tipped her head back until his intensely blue eyes filled her world. Then his lips were on hers, soft and insistent.

The wonder of their first kiss—that it was happening at all—made Isabelle cease to think, cease to move, to breathe, to stop everything except to feel that kiss upon her lips. He pressed gently, not too insistently, but enough that she understood he wanted to claim her as his. Almost as though he sought to taste her, his tongue darted out, licking along her bottom lip, making her shiver. Making her feel tingles all over her body, even down in her—

Isabelle jumped back, heat rushing to her cheeks. That tingling had never happened to her before, especially not in her private place. Was that supposed to happen?

"Isabelle?" Frank concern on Sandy's face made her doubt it even more. "What's the matter, sweetheart?"

She mustn't alarm him but she couldn't let him know what had happened either. She smiled and shook her head. "Nothing, I just…no, nothing is wrong." Heat scorched her cheeks. "I've just never…been kissed like that before."

He grinned, looking like a wicked imp. "Well, I hope you liked it, or will come to like it very quickly." He leaned forward and whispered, "Because I intend to do it quite a lot in the future."

"Sandy!" The fire in her cheeks threatened to burst into flame. Stepping back quickly, she lost her balance and he grabbed her to keep her from falling. He pulled her upright and they came face to face, where he proceeded to stare at her mouth hungrily.

"Time for lesson number two."

Before she could protest, his mouth was on hers again, more insistent this time, pressing against her more firmly, making her squirm as the tingles erupted all over again. Good lord, what was he doing to her?

"Ahem."

At the sound, they jumped apart so quickly Isabelle stumbled into a chair and sat down hard. Her gaze shot toward the door, where the noise had come from to find a stranger, a gentleman in evening clothes to be exact, entering the room and shutting the door.

"Yule, for God's sake." Sandy ran a hand through his hair,

then shook his head and laughed.

Isabelle slumped in the chair. Obviously, the gentleman was known to Sandy, so that should be all right. They were, after all, betrothed. Still, she was very glad it hadn't been Ambrose who had found them in such a compromising position.

"A good thing I happened to see you and Miss Devereaux come in here or I'd be looking for you yet." The tall gentleman frowned. "You should not be in here by yourselves, no matter how innocent the reason." He glanced at Isabelle and bowed. "I assume you were telling the young lady about her list of dance partners for the evening."

Sandy smiled ruefully as he held out his hand to Isabelle.

She took it and rose, his rock-solid strength reassuring her.

"Yes, I have given Miss Devereaux her dance card and was about to seek you out to introduce you to her before your dance." He led her over to the dark-haired gentleman, who had the same look about his eyes as Sandy. "Miss Devereaux, may I introduce my cousin, Mr. Ulysses Quartermain who is to be your next partner. Yule, this is Miss Isabelle Devereaux..." Sandy grinned and squeezed her hand. "My fiancée."

Mr. Quartermain stepped back, his astonished face making Isabelle giggle. "Good lord, Sandy. You never mentioned that when you asked me to partner the young lady."

"Because it hadn't happened yet." Sandy continued to gaze into her eyes so deeply, she could feel herself falling into them. "It was only just now that she made me the happiest man in the world."

"Then please allow me to be the first to wish you every happiness, Miss Devereaux. Congratulations, cousin. I see the rest of us are going to have to get on and fulfil our part of the wager as well." Mr. Quartermain stopped abruptly and turned a wary eye on Sandy. "Does she know about ...our circumstances, Sandy?"

Puzzled, Isabelle frowned at Sandy. What circumstances did *he* have to consider?

But her intended merely nodded, unconcerned. "Yes, in fact,

cuz. I informed her early in our acquaintanceship about the marriage wager."

Oh, *that* circumstance. The wager. So caught up in her own scandal, she'd completely forgotten about his family's wager to get all the cousins married. A silly thing, but if it had played a part in Sandy wishing to marry her, all the better.

"Have you set a date yet?" Yule looked from Sandy to Isabelle.

For herself she'd do it tomorrow if the law allowed it. Still, the sooner the better for her. "Could we do it by the end of the week, my lord?"

Both gentlemen turned startled eyes on her. Rightly so, she supposed. The custom of the day was to have at least a six month engagement, with a big Society wedding at the end of it. All Isabelle wanted to do was to be married as soon as possible and beyond the reach of her stepfather.

"Isabelle." Sandy, who had dropped her hands, now gathered them together again. "We don't need to rush quite so much, do we, my dear?"

"Is there a particular reason you wish to marry so swiftly, Miss Devereaux?" Mr. Quartermain looked askance at his cousin. "Sandy? Don't tell me something has already occurred—"

"No, Yule." Sandy put a hand up to stop his cousin's embarrassing question before he could get it out. "There is no reason of that nature to speed the wedding, I assure you." He glanced at Isabelle. "Although there is a very good reason for haste." He stared at Isabelle and raised an eyebrow, asking permission.

Well, his cousin would now be part of her family, so he might as well know. She nodded.

"Miss Devereaux is concerned about her stepfather's temper, Yule. In the past, it has gotten the better of him and he was…exceedingly unkind to her and her mother. Isabelle would like to be married and out of the house as soon as possible." He lifted her hands and kissed them. "I am sorry I didn't think of that earlier, my dear. I can apply for a special license tomorrow. If I cannot procure it, my grandfather will be able to. He is very persuasive."

His cousin nodded. "You should enlist Grandfather's help immediately. He will wish to know about the wedding at any rate and facilitate it if he can. Today is the twenty-second of September. Let us name October first as the wedding day. That gives some little time to pull together a hasty wedding."

"Like Alex's." Sandy didn't sound happy about that. "I was hoping we could avoid that particular similarity, but perhaps quick weddings will be the Quartermain trademark."

"I don't mind, Sandy," Isabelle whispered to him.

"You should have the largest, most elaborate wedding imaginable, my love. But I know the reason for your need for haste. We will have to compensate by having a prolonged honeymoon."

Isabelle swallowed hard but managed a smile. She'd have a week to prepare herself, to arrange a small wedding and then tell her mother and Ambrose at the very last minute. There were so many arrangements to see to, not the least of which would be persuading Grace and her mother to allow her to be married from their home. It was a lot to ask, but it must be done. She wanted Ambrose to know nothing of her escape until it was a *fait accompli*. Then there would be no way for him to stop her marriage, no way to prevent her final escape from him as she fled into the arms of the man she loved.

CHAPTER EIGHT

London
October 1

STANDING AT THE temporary altar, Sandy gazed around the ballroom in his grandfather's townhouse, the polished floors shining for the first time since Sandy had been a boy. Once their children all married, his grandparents had refused to entertain in Town, preferring instead to host a house party each year at their primary country estate for the family. Last week, however, Sandy had persuaded Grandfather that his wedding was important enough to open up the townhouse, providing a place for Sandy and Isabelle to be wed.

Even after that hurdle had been overcome, they almost hadn't managed to pull it off.

Isabelle had been insistent that her mother and stepfather not be informed about the wedding until the last moment. She'd persuaded Sandy that her mother had given tacit permission for the marriage by allowing her to meet with Sandy at Mrs. Hatch's because they hoped he would propose soon. Unfortunately, Isabelle had been outwitted, when Grandfather had insisted the settlements be negotiated for her. He would not budge on the question. As Captain Grey was Isabelle's legal guardian, he must be informed of the impending marriage so he could act in

Isabelle's best interests.

The ensuing argument between Isabelle, her mother, and Captain Grey had shown Sandy in no uncertain terms how stubborn his bride-to-be could be. Her mother pled for a six-month engagement—she got five days. Mrs. Grey insisted they be married at St. Georges. Isabelle instead asked Mrs. Horton if they could be married from her house. Grace had been such a true friend, offering Isabelle shelter the entire week of her engagement, she insisted Grace be her bridesmaid. They had had fun the entire time preparing for the wedding.

Her mother, however, kept insisting on a church wedding for her only daughter. Isabelle had dug in her heels until finally a compromise had been reached when Sandy had offered his grandfather's townhouse. The residence of a duke seemed to placate Mrs. Grey and the plans hurried on apace after that.

Now the few guests attending—Captain and Mrs. Grey, Mrs. Horton, all of Sandy's cousins and their wives, his mother, and his grandparents—were seated at one end of the ballroom in rows of chairs before an altar that mimicked a church's nave. At the opposite end, tables groaned under laden platters of food awaiting the wedding breakfast.

Sandy glanced at Yule, acting as his best man, shooting him a nervous grin. He'd be so thankful once this ordeal was all over. After all the controversy over the wedding, Sandy was impatient to have it finished. Impatient to have Isabelle safe and secure as his wife. Even more impatient to be able to take his wife to bed on their wedding night and show her how much he truly loved her. Base thought though it might be, Sandy doubted no groom ever thought otherwise.

He turned expectantly at movement from the doorway and caught his breath. Grace had already entered the ballroom, with Isabelle directly behind. The sight of her made him weak.

Dressed in a gold and white gown he'd seen her wear several times before—there had been no time to bespeak a wedding gown—Isabelle nevertheless looked stunning as she walked sedately down the makeshift aisle toward him. The candlelight caught the strands of gold in the multiple layers of the gown, dazzling Sandy as though the light itself was coming toward him. Her thin veil barely hid her face, but he could imagine the broad smile on her lips beneath it.

She had managed to get exactly what she wanted for her wedding—including no escort down the aisle. Others might think it strange, but Sandy and Mrs. Grey understood all too well. At least, after the next half-hour or so, Isabelle need never worry about experiencing violence at the hand of her monster of a stepfather ever again.

Grace had reached him and stood off to the side. Then Isabelle stood at his side, and Grace lifted her veil. The exquisite beauty of his bride's face—the dark brows swooping up above inky lashes and deep sapphire eyes in a smooth pale face with deep pink cupid's bow lips—sent a unexpected shiver of lust all throughout Sandy until he had to swallow hard to control himself.

Of course, he'd imagined what it would be like to have Isabelle beneath him in his bed. Hell, he'd begun imagining that almost from the moment he met her. But now, to have her so close to being his, he found his riotous flesh didn't want to wait another minute. If this urgent desire to feel her body underneath his didn't subside, they might actually have to cut the breakfast short and retire to one of his grandfather's guest chambers. Scandalous, but he didn't care at this point.

He drew a long breath to settle himself and took Isabelle's hand. The touch of her slender fingers, even through gloves, sent an erotic shock through his body. Only a few more minutes. He could last a few more minutes if he concentrated.

The Reverend Mr. Buckelew opened his Book of Common Prayer and began to read the familiar marriage service. "Dearly beloved friends, we are gathered together here in the sight of God..."

Gazing deeply into Isabelle's eyes, Sandy's happiness soared as if on wings. They were going to have the perfect life together, despite the obstacles that had tried to prevent it. Their marriage would be like that of his own parents—two people who adored one another, who would cherish and support each other, not only because of the unbreakable bonds of matrimony, but by the even stronger bonds of love.

Mr. Buckelew gave him his charge of intent and he answered quickly and loudly, "I will." A chuckle rose from the section where his cousins were sitting, but he paid them no mind. They were almost there. He listened eagerly as the reverend asked Isabelle the same charge, "Will thou have this man to be thy wedded husband?"

For a long moment Isabelle hesitated, her eyes searching his, as though seeking an answer to an unspoken question. She then turned her head to gaze into the congregation, at her mother, perhaps? Or was it Captain Grey? When she turned back to him, a tiny tear welled in her eyes, spilled over, and trickled down her cheek. "I…I…"

She bent her head and gave a quiet sob. "I…cannot." Raising her head, she gazed into his face again—a face that had frozen into a stunned mask of disbelief. "I'm so sorry, Sandy. But I simply cannot."

Uncomprehending, Sandy automatically squeezed her hand. What was she saying? "Isabelle?"

With a heart-wrenching sob, Isabelle tore her hand from his, picked up her skirts, and fled back down the aisle and out the ballroom door.

Unable to move, as though he'd been nailed to the floor, Sandy could only watch her go, shaking his head as if to deny the evidence of his own eyes.

Isabelle was gone.

A deafening chatter erupted from the wedding guests, but Sandy scarcely heard them. His gaze had fixed on the doorway through which his bride—his beloved Isabelle—had fled from him.

"Sandy. Sandy!" A rough hand seized his shoulder and he was abruptly spun around to face an irate Yule. "What the hell is going on?"

Still barely aware of anything, save the knowledge Isabelle had left him, Sandy shrugged. "I don't know."

Suddenly, he was inundated with people jostling him, everyone trying to get close enough to demand the same questions over and over again.

"What happened? Where did she go?"

"I don't know."

"Where is Isabelle?"

"I don't know."

"What happened, Sandy?"

"I don't know."

"Why did Isabelle run away?"

"I don't know!" He wrenched himself away from his mother, who had asked that last question. He would go mad if this questioning didn't stop. "Can someone go look for her?" His gaze fell on Grace, whose stricken face was wet with tears. She sniffed, nodded, and hurried from the room.

"What is the meaning of this, Lord MacKay?" Captain Grey had shoved his way to the front of the group of concerned guests clustered around Sandy. "What did you do to make Isabelle run away like that?"

"What did *I* do?" Sandy wheeled around on the larger gentleman, his blood heating instantly. "I might ask the same of you, sir. It is *you* she was fleeing."

"Indeed? It appeared to me as though she sought to escape you, my lord." The smirk on Grey's face was the last straw for Sandy. He drew back and let fly a right hook Langham himself would have been proud of.

The captain stumbled backward and would have come for Sandy had Alex and Julius not restrained him. Yule grabbed Sandy by the arm as well. "Don't feed what is easily going to be the scandal of the week, cuz."

Sandy had shaken off Yule's grip, almost deciding to go for Grey again anyway, when Grace hurried back into the ballroom. "My lord, she's gone."

"Gone?" Sandy held up a hand as Yule attempted to grab his arm. "What do you mean? Gone where?"

"I'm not sure, my lord. I searched for her on this floor and asked a maid if she'd seen a lady on the first floor, but she said no. Then I went to the entryway and found the butler. He said she'd run out the door and flung herself into the carriage." Grace gulped. "The one you and Isabelle were supposed to set off in for your wedding trip."

Sandy ran his hand through his hair. "Where might she go, Grace?"

"Home, my lord?"

Sandy shook his head vehemently. He'd not believe that unless he saw it with his own eyes. "No, there must be somewhere else."

"Perhaps she's gone back to Miss Horton's home, Sandy." Yule's steady voice was a godsend. "Let's take my carriage. I'll tell the others."

Nodding, Sandy bowed to the still trembling Grace, who bobbed a curtsy and ran off toward the ballroom. He then headed to the foyer, bent on finding a place to hide himself until Yule arrived. In no mood to engage with any of his relations, who would likely be trooping through here any minute, Sandy headed into a small receiving room on the right. The waiting was interminable, but at last Yule popped his head in. "Let's go."

As they settled themselves into the comfortable leather seats of the carriage, Sandy noticed the conveyances for his other relations still present in and around the front of the townhouse. "Didn't anyone leave?"

"Only Captain and Mrs. Grey. All our relations have fallen on the wedding breakfast for consolation and sustenance."

"Vultures."

"Birds of prey, perhaps. The cousins wanted to keep up their strength in the event they were needed. After the punch you dealt Grey, I thought they might have a point." Yule peered at him. "How are you holding up?"

"Not well, Yule. Not well at all." Sandy dropped his head in his hands, squeezing it until the pounding in his brain eased a trifle. "I have no idea why she would have done this. She got her way in everything to do with the wedding." Wrack his brain though he might, he could devise no reason whatsoever why Isabelle would have deserted him.

"I expect when you find her, it will have all been some trivial misunderstanding."

Sandy stared at his cousin with a baleful eye. "No bride would jilt her groom at the altar over something trivial. Besides..." Sandy ground his teeth. "She wanted to marry me. She needed to marry me to escape her stepfather. I cannot think how that might have changed between last night and this morning."

"Escape Captain Grey? But he's just returned." Yule's frown had a touch of impatience about it.

"That is the trouble. Remember, I told you he'd been unkind to Isabelle and her mother?"

By the time Sandy had finished the tale of Captain Grey's violence toward his wife and stepdaughter, they were drawing up in front of the Horton's residence. Sandy was out of the carriage and banging on the front door before the horses had come to a halt.

A flustered maid opened the door.

"Is Miss Devereaux here?" The desperation in Sandy's voice must have frightened the girl, because she stepped back and put her hands up as if to fend him off.

"Oh, no, m'lord. She left early this morning to be married to Lord MacKay. My mistress said it was to take place at Welwyn House in Mayfair. That's a duke's house, if you don't know it." The maid's eyes widened, her mouth popping open. "Are you trying to stop the wedding, m'lord?"

"No, I'm trying to make sure it takes place. Thank you."

Sandy turned away, so frustrated he chewed his lip. He headed back to the carriage, thinking hard. Where else might Isabelle have gone?

"Not here, I take it?" Yule opened the door and Sandy climbed in, trying to puzzle it out.

"No, and my mind is about to burst into a thousand pieces with all the possibilities running through my brain. Why did she run and where did she run to?"

"She has no other friends she might go to?"

"None I know of save Grace. She was a very solitary woman, Yule, and rightly so." There must be a piece of the puzzle he simply didn't have.

"No friends here in Town, but what about her home? Mrs. Grey doesn't reside in London, does she, outside of the Season?" Yule's excitement threatened to leap to Sandy.

"I think not. Isabelle didn't dwell on her younger life, except for the cruelties visited on her by her stepfather. Still, you may have hit upon something, cousin." Sandy rapped on the trap. "Twenty-seven Ormond Yard, please," he shouted up. "There may very well be information about either their friends at home or here in London with which Mrs. Grey hasn't been forthcoming."

"Well, you did just punch her husband."

"She might thank me for that, actually. Sauce for the goose, you know."

When they arrived, to Sandy's surprise, Yule jumped down to accompany him.

"In case Captain Grey is in the habit of holding a grudge," was all he would say.

Sandy knocked and was shown into the same small parlor as he had been all these weeks.

Moments later, Mrs. Grey rushed into the room, her face pale, her brows furrowed. "Have you found her?" she whispered.

"No." Sandy automatically lowered his voice as well. "I came to ask if you have any idea where else she could have gone? Back to your home town, perhaps? Did she have friends there?"

The lady shook her head and looked as if she might swoon.

"Please, ma'am, sit." Yule led her to a delicate sofa and sat her down. "Your daughter had no friends growing up? No childhood companions?"

Her face pinched, Mrs. Grey shook her head in quick little jerks. "Not in Kent. She wasn't encouraged to play with other children after I remarried."

"What about before that, during your first marriage to Isabelle's father?" Sandy could have cursed himself for not finding out more about Isabelle's early life. She'd encouraged him to talk about his family and friends and he'd happily obliged, without seeking many details about her in return.

"Oh, that is when we lived in the North, in Carlisle. That was Mr. Devereaux's home." Mrs. Grey peered around, as if afraid someone might overhear her. "We lived there on his estate until his tragic death when Isabelle was ten. His mother is still there, Isabelle's grandmother, although she's old and infirm."

"And is she Isabelle's only other relation?" Sandy shot a glance to Yule, who shrugged.

"Yes, there's no one else."

"Then that must be it." Sandy's heart surged with hope.

"Doubtful." Yule shook his head. "If her grandmother lives so far away, it's unlikely Isabelle would have had the means to take a train, much less a carriage, on such short notice. Where would she get the funds?" Yule had remained in the doorway, his arms crossed over his chest. Every so often, he'd glance over his shoulder into the corridor, as if to check to see if anyone was coming. So far, Captain Grey had not put in an appearance.

"That is true." Her mother hung her head. "In any case, I doubt Isabelle would attempt to make that long journey by herself."

Sandy wasn't so sure of that.

"And as you say, she would not have had funds with her…Oh!" Mrs. Grey's hand went to her throat, staring at Sandy intently. "I suggested she take a purse of gold coins with her, to throw from the carriage as you drove through the city streets. A celebration, you know."

Sandy and Yule exchanged a look.

"If she did take money with her…"

"Then more than likely, she's on her way to Carlisle this minute." Sandy was torn between anger and worry that she had done something so foolhardy as to travel alone, and relief that he'd finally discovered where Isabelle had gone. "We'll go check the train station now."

"The last train north left half an hour ago." Yule snapped to attention. "And I believe I hear your husband approaching, madam." He grabbed Sandy's shoulder and they turned to go.

Almost out the door, Sandy turned back to the pale woman weeping on the sofa. "Do you have any idea, ma'am why she would have run from me?"

The little woman shook her head and stared at him, utterly defeated. "She was running toward you, my lord. Toward an escape to a better life. What changed her mind, I cannot imagine."

"Sandy." Yule tipped his head toward the front door and Sandy left. He didn't understand why Isabelle had run any more than her mother. But when he finally reached her, he would bloody well find out.

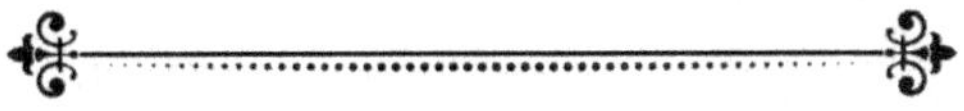

CHAPTER NINE

Carlisle, England
October 2

THE COZY PARLOR in her Grandmother Devereaux's manor house—the house Isabelle had been born and grew up in until she was ten years old—on the outskirts of Carlisle had always seemed a place of refuge during the years after her father died, when her mother moved them to London. She'd been allowed to visit once each year, until Mama married Ambrose. Since then, she'd thought about her grandmother's house often, a refuge when things got truly bad at home. It certainly had proved a blessing now.

She and Grandmama sat before a warm fire taking tea and discussing everything but the most obvious questions—what had happened and what was she going to do now? Isabelle had turned up on the doorstep last evening, surprising her grandmother, who took the news that her granddaughter had jilted her fiancé and was here without clothes or money in her stride. Today Grandmama had the bedchambers searched for cast-off clothing, gathering a motley group of garments that would have to serve her granddaughter for the moment. Now, Isabelle feared, her grandmother would demand to be told what was going on. That story was going to be difficult for many reasons, not the least of which was that each time she thought about Sandy and the life they might have had, she tuned up to cry.

"Will Captain Grey acquire another ship and set sail once more?" Grandmama sipped her special blend of Oolong and Congou black tea with milk and plenty of sugar.

"I'm sorry, but I don't know, Grandmama. Once he appeared in London, I took care to stay as far away from him as possible." Isabelle took a small sip of tea. Her stomach had been roiling ever since she ran from the duke's townhouse. She'd scarcely eaten anything since she arrived in Carlisle, save tea and toast. "I can only pray he does, for Mama's sake as well as mine. I will not return to London until he has gone."

"I hope that is possible, my dear. You know you are welcome here as long as you live. Indeed, the property will come to you upon my death. But as you have not yet reached your majority, I cannot legally keep you from him, much as I would wish to." She sniffed. "If only I possessed a weapon, I'd make certain the man could never lay a hand on you again." Her grandmother was one of the only people Isabelle had confided in about her stepfather's brutality. "I haven't shot a gun in years, but I remember how to pull the trigger well enough."

"I should be fine hidden here for a while. They do not know where I have gone, so they will not come looking for me. Especially not all the way up here. I'm praying night and day that he will simply ride his wave of notoriety until he can set sail again. Certainly it will be too much trouble to journey all the way up here just for me." Unfortunately, she didn't believe that in the least.

"Some men seek absolute control over a woman." Grandmama pursed her lips, then took a sip of tea. "Those are the ones like your stepfather who feel threatened by women. It is not enough for them to have legal control. They must punish them physically as well, to persuade themselves they are master in their house." The old woman shook her head, her face a dark frown. "How your mother went from my son, who would have died rather than harm a woman, to this heartless beast is unimaginable." She raised her cup to her lips, then set it down again. "I would not be surprised if your father's death didn't unhinge Miranda's mind. I see no other explanation for her to marry Grey."

So many things would have been different had Papa not succumbed to cholera eight years ago. She remembered her father with so much love. A kind, funny, and loving man. Very much like… A chill shivered down Isabelle's spine. She refused to think about Lord MacKay now. After her unexpected appearance, she'd told her grandmother something of her courtship with Sandy and the abandoned wedding. After that brief explanation, she'd refused to speak of him. She didn't want to think of him, or what might have been, had circumstances been different.

"In the event Captain Grey does come here to take me back to London, we must have a plan to hide me, because I will not go back with him, Grandmama." The mere thought of going anywhere with Ambrose Grey set Isabelle into a panic. "Is there somewhere you can send me, some place he'd never think to look?" Desperation welled up inside her, making her shake until her teacup rattled in its saucer. "We must think, Grandmama."

"There's a gentleman at the door, ma'am."

Isabelle's cup and saucer crashed to the floor. The maid had opened the door so softly, Isabelle hadn't heard her until she spoke.

"Who is this gentleman, Davis? Let the cup alone." Her grandmother was brooking no nonsense today. "Did he give a name?"

"He asked after Miss Devereaux, ma'am. I didn't ask his name."

"Is…is it a tall gentleman, Davis?" Isabelle rose, determined to take flight if need be.

"No, miss. A shorter gentleman, only a little taller than yourself." She turned her attention to her mistress. "Is that all, ma'am? Shall I fetch him in?"

Isabelle sat back down, relief pouring through her. *Not Ambrose.* Then she shot up in her seat. If not her stepfather, then it could only be… "Sandy."

Grandmother looked inordinately pleased. "I told you your young gentleman would come for you." Then to the maid, she said, "Show him in, Davis."

"But, Grandmama—"

Her grandmother's eyes bored into her, until Isabelle had to look away. "No, Isabelle. If he has taken the trouble to follow you all the way up here, he deserves an audience."

Much to her dismay, she knew Grandmama was right. That did not make the situation any less painful, however. Isabelle hung her head and braced herself.

The door opened again and Sandy…no, Lord MacKay, entered, his mien sober. The smiling, friendly, helpful gentleman she'd depended on had gone, leaving only a man who looked as though he expected her to pull a knife and stab him in the heart. Perhaps that was what she'd already done.

The whole journey up to Carlisle she'd tried to prepare herself for this inevitable meeting, tried to maintain a cool, calm demeanor. She might as well have saved herself the trouble. Her heart took off beating so hard, she feared he could hear it. He looked so distant, his dark suit giving him a stark look she'd never seen before and didn't much like. It was too severe for the kind man she'd wanted to marry. She feared that kindness had gone for good.

He bowed to her. "Miss Devereaux." He clipped the syllables of her name so sharply, she scarcely recognized it. Glancing to her grandmother, his face softened and Isabelle took heart a little. "Would you be so kind as to introduce me to your grandmother?"

Trying to hide her trembling, Isabelle rose. "Grandmama, may I introduce Lord MacKay, of Carnwath. My lord, my grandmother, Mrs. Devereaux."

"Delighted to meet you, ma'am." He executed a short bow

flawlessly. "Despite the circumstances, I bring you best wishes from Mrs. Grey." He turned to Isabelle, his face hardening. "She sends her regards to you as well, Isabelle, although she has been terribly worried about you. As we all have."

That was fair. As she hadn't wanted to reveal her whereabouts to her stepfather, she'd refused to send word to her mother. The telegram she'd received from her yesterday had gone unanswered.

"I am sorry for your trouble, my lord. I had good reason to conceal my location from Captain Grey, as you well know. I am sorry if my mother is worried, but I did what I thought best."

"You thought it best to let me believe you loved me, Isabelle? That you wished to marry me? How was it best to leave me at the altar without a single word to tell me why?" The pain in his face tied her heart in knots.

She'd done what she'd thought best for both of them in making a clean break. Perhaps she'd been wrong in that. She suspected she'd find out in their coming conversation.

"I am very pleased to meet you, Lord MacKay." Grandmama rose stiffly. She waved away Sandy's offer of assistance and reached for her cane. "I will leave you two to your discussion. I am certain you will both find illumination by the end of it." Making her way slowly to the door, Grandmama kept her gaze on Lord MacKay. "I will say this, Isabelle." She paused at the threshold. "You have excellent taste in gentlemen."

Heat raced to Isabelle's face and she fervently wished it were permissible to upbraid one's elders in public.

As if she could hear her granddaughter's thoughts, Grandmama went out the door with a chuckle, closing it behind her.

"I like your grandmother." Sandy crossed to the chair opposite Isabelle and sat. "She puts me in mind of my mother. No nonsense and right to the point." He continued to stare at Isabelle, making her dread the coming conversation even more.

"I have traveled a long way to ask you a single question, Isabelle. I ask only that you give me a true answer to it."

Slowly, she nodded. She owed him that at least. Still, she'd put it off as long as she could. "Would you like some tea?"

An exasperated sigh escaped him, but he nodded. "Yes, please. Milk and—"

"Two lumps. I remember." Hand shaking, she took up the teapot and poured carefully, taking her time as she plopped in the lumps, then added the milk until it was the exact shade he liked. Drawing out the time before she must explain herself—and lose Sandy forever—she handed him the cup, took a deep breath to steady herself, then clasped her hands in her lap. "What did you wish to ask me, my lord?"

Taking his time, Sandy sipped his tea, his gaze squarely on her. After what seemed an eternity, he set the cup down and leaned forward. "Did you never love me at all, Isabelle? Was I completely wrong in believing you did? Was I truly only a means to an end for you?"

Stunned, Isabelle stared at him, trying to open her mouth, trying to form an answer to the last question she'd been expecting. She'd been prepared for "Why did you leave?" But this question…well, there was only one truthful answer she could give, painful as it was. "I did love you, Sandy. I do love you still. If you will believe anything, believe that. How could I not fall in love with someone so kind, so generous, so…good?"

As though she'd uttered magic words, he puffed out a breath he'd been holding, the charming smile she loved so much spreading across his face. "Thank God, Isabelle." He seized her hand and kissed it, sending a streak of warmth all the way to her heart. "You cannot know the agony I've been in all this time, thinking I'd done something to upset you. Something that…I don't know, reminded you of your stepfather, although I couldn't imagine what it could have been." He stopped, dropped his gaze from hers. "You will likely hear of this when we return to London, but I will tell you myself. I punched Captain Grey just after you left my grandfather's house."

"You punched Ambrose?" Shocked, Isabelle forgot her nervousness. "You really hit him?"

"I did." He sniggered. "Gave him a knock so hard, blood flew."

"I wish I could have seen that." Isabelle closed her eyes, savoring the image of her stepfather bleeding on the ballroom floor. Small compensation perhaps, but at least she was assured he knew what it felt like to be beaten and humiliated.

"So why, Isabelle?" Sandy cradled her cheek with a gentle hand. "Why did you abandon me?"

Drawing his hand away, she grasped it instead, needing all the strength she could get for the coming confession. "Because I love you, Sandy." The confusion on his face smote her, but she forced herself to continue. "Because I finally realized I couldn't marry you without telling you the whole truth about myself."

"The whole truth?" His brows furrowed, darkening his handsome face.

"About…my stepfather." Isabelle had to bite back the gorge that rose in her throat. She would rather walk over hot coals than to confess this to Sandy, but she must do it. At the very least, she owed him that.

His thunderous look darkened further, if that was even possible, transforming his usual genial visage into that of a terrifying imp from hell. He squeezed her hands unmercifully. "What about him?"

Unable to look him in the eyes any longer, Isabelle dropped her gaze to their clenched hands. "I told you he beat me and my mother and that was true. He did that for many years." Hot tears pricked her eyes. Oh, but she had hoped not to cry in front of him, although soon it would make no difference what she did. "But the last week before he sailed on the *Cordelia*, he…found a new way to hurt me."

"Isabelle?"

She risked a glance at Sandy and immediately wished she hadn't. His face had drained of color and drawn in on itself, the lines deepened as though suddenly etched with the sharpest knife.

Yet she must continue. There was nothing else she could do. "One night after I'd gone to bed, I heard him arguing with my mother, heard her cries when he hit her repeatedly. Then the house became quiet, and I prayed he'd gone out or fallen asleep. But just as I'd begun to relax, the door to my bedroom opened. I braced myself to be pulled out of bed and whipped—he used a leather belt and made me count the strokes as they fell."

"Dear God." The utter horror on Sandy's face made her cringe.

"But that night, he didn't have the belt with him. Instead, he unbuttoned his fly and lowered his trousers…" Isabelle hung her head, unable to go on. That scene had played itself out in her mind over and over for more than a year after the nightly visits to her bed ceased, stopped only because he left to go to sea.

"Oh, my dear." His soft, consoling voice broke her.

She burst into tears, sobbing as she'd not been able to since it had happened to the terrified fifteen-year-old Isabelle, violated and all alone in her ravaged bed. Crying also for the Isabelle who wanted so very badly to be loved by this kind, generous man, but who had known that could never happen once the truth came out, as it now had.

All of a sudden, she found herself cradled in his arms, held tightly against his chest. Her tears redoubled. He was so incredibly kind, so compassionate, toward her. The best man in the world, really. And she could have been his wife, could have had this love for all of her life, had her mother never married the monstrous Ambrose Grey.

At last she seemed to have cried herself out, the tears drying to a trickle, all swallowed up by the soft superfine of Sandy's jacket. Panting to get her breath she sat up, as ready as she'd ever be to finish answering his question. "So you see, I've been living a lie these past three years. Pretending that I would be an eligible *parti* for the marriage mart when I turned eighteen. I never told anyone what had happened, not even Mama. With Ambrose presumed dead, there seemed no real need."

"And there were no further…consequences?"

"No, praise God. Nothing changed…except I was changed. I stopped thinking that I would some day marry. No man would want me after discovering I wasn't an innocent. I tried to tell Mama I wasn't ready to get married, but I couldn't put her off without telling her why. Then she coaxed me into coming to London for the Season and then staying for the Little Season. I'd hoped if I showed her how ill at ease I was, she wouldn't make me return next year. So I consented to dance at some of the entertainments, thinking in November we'd quietly return to Kent, but then…"

"Then I stepped in and saved you from Barclay." Sandy smiled ruefully.

"Yes, you did. I tried to get rid of you as well, but you were too—"

"Persistent." He grinned. "A Quartermain trait."

"You were so kind, so clever." Isabelle couldn't look at him or her heart would break in two. "I began to hope that perhaps you might be different, might be the one gentleman who would understand what happened to me wasn't my fault. The one who might be able to love me despite the fact I was ruined."

"Why didn't you tell me all this before the wedding, my love?"

The endearment cut like a knife twisted in her heart.

"Because I thought if I did, I would lose you. All I could think was that I needed to escape Ambrose—I couldn't allow him to…hurt me that way again. I had to get away and the only hope I had was to marry you." She wiped her eyes again. So there were still tears to be shed. "I'm so sorry I tried to deceive you. And glad I couldn't do it in the end." Cupping his cheek, she gazed longingly into his face, the one she wanted to see every day for the rest of her life. "When I looked into your eyes when you were saying your vows, I knew I'd been lying to myself, and that could be forgiven. However, I couldn't lie to you, Sandy. All I could do to make it right was run away." Dropping her hand, Isabelle hung her head. "Please, don't despise me."

Defeated, she sat silently, waiting for him to leave.

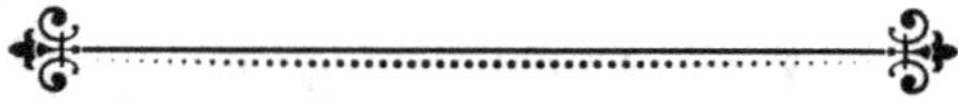

Chapter Ten

As if all the air in the room had been sucked out, Sandy couldn't breathe. Long before Isabelle's woeful tale had taken its sudden hideous turn, he'd concluded Captain Ambrose Grey had to die. Once she revealed the extent of Grey's depravity, the man's fate was all but sealed. He'd wanted to kill him when Isabelle first told him of the abuse, but had put it off for another day. That day had now come. When Sandy returned to London, he'd challenge Grey and shoot him down like the rabid dog he was. Duels might belong to a bygone era, but if he sullied the man's name badly enough, he'd be forced to fight or be branded a coward. Sandy fisted his hand, imagining it held a pistol aimed at Grey's midsection. No clean shot to the heart for that monster. No, a wound to his bowels that would fester, causing him to sicken and suffer in excruciating pain for days still was not punishment enough. It wouldn't compare to the pain Isabelle had endured these past years, but it would have to suffice.

The sound of weeping brought him back to himself, to discover poor Isabelle crying quietly beside him. Now who was being an insensitive brute?

"Isabelle?" He slid his arms around her, thinking to comfort her, but she only cried harder, her body shaking uncontrollably. At a loss to know what else to do to ease her pain, and suspecting nothing could, he elected to simply hold her tightly until her grief subsided.

He couldn't pretend to know how horribly her stepfather's perfidy had hurt her, both physically and deep in her soul. Wounds of that sort might take a lifetime to heal. His greatest fear, however, was that they might never do so.

At last he wrapped his arms around her more fiercely and whispered, "I know you are upset that you have had to make this confession to me, my dear. But when you have got yourself in hand, we do need to talk."

She sputtered a little more, sniffed, then finally took a deep breath. Red-faced, eyes swollen, she turned her head away and mumbled, "I must go."

When she tried to rise however, she couldn't. He held onto her firmly, not about to let her flee. "You are fine where you are, Isabelle."

"I look an absolute fright, my lord. I need to put cold water on my face." She continued to hide it from him, though he didn't care a tuppence about how she looked at the moment.

"My lord? Do not tell me you are reneging on your promise to use my first name, Miss Devereaux?"

"I shouldn't call you by your first name, my lord." She still hid her face from him, which made everything more difficult.

"Have I given you any indication I wished for us to be formal with one another again? To discontinue our warmer relationship?"

Slowly, she turned her face toward him, streaks of tears still on her cheeks. She looked so woebegone, his heart hurt with wanting to make her smile once more. "No, you have not, but you are kind, my lord. You have been like an angel, keeping me from harm. You take pity on me now and wish not to upset me, when by all rights you should distance yourself from me." She sniffed and he feared the tears would begin to flow again. "As should everyone."

He seized her hands again, chafing her cold fingers. "Why would I wish to distance myself from the woman I love? The only woman in the world I wish to call my wife?"

Disbelief made her face pinched and miserable.

Undeterred, he pressed his lips to her wet cheek. "Oh, Isabelle, can you not trust me to know that what he did to you was never your fault?"

Slowly, she shook her head, her eyes still wary. "You cannot mean that, my—"

He screwed his face into a thunderous frown.

"Sandy," she said quickly.

"I most certainly do, my love." He sighed and leaned his forehead against hers. "I know, given the circumstances, you cannot trust men as you otherwise might have. But I beg of you, sweetheart, trust me." He wrapped his arms all the way around her, never wanting to let her go. "If I have not said it plainly before, I say it now. I love you, Isabelle. I want you to be my wife and the mother of my children. Only you, my love."

"Oh, Sandy." Her countenance softened, her eyes pleading with him. "I do want to believe that with all my heart. But Society will not tolerate such a thing, my dear. A ruined woman is never accepted by the *ton*."

"But you are not ruined in their eyes, my dear. No one knows but you, me, and your stepfather. As long as he stays silent, you have nothing to fear." It certainly gave Grey power over them, but it was a chance they had to take.

"When I thought him dead, I knew the secret was safe, but now..." Isabelle bit her bottom lip. "I may never be safe again. What if he tells someone?"

"Who can he tell without implicating himself? How else would he know?" Sandy drew a long breath. "After we are married, it will be a moot point, because I will swear to anyone who asks that you were a virgin on our wedding night."

"Sandy!" That seemed to take the wind out of her sails. "You can't mean you would lie about it."

"I do mean it, Isabelle."

"But I'm not...a virgin," she whispered and hung her head.

He seized her face in both hands and stared at her until she returned his gaze. "You will be a virgin to me, my love. We will not dwell on what he took from you, only on what we will share together. I promise to be the gentlest and most loving of husbands, if you will still have me."

A ray of hope shone in Isabelle's eyes for the first time today. "And you're perfectly sure, Sandy?"

At last, she'd given him an inkling that everything would come right. "I love you, Isabelle. More each time I behold your lovely face. There is nothing anyone could ever say to me that would make me love you less." Gazing into all that beauty, he could avow he loved her more with each breath he took. Now he needed to show her, irrevocably, he meant what he said.

He slipped off the sofa and onto the floor, going down on one knee, and grasping her hand. "Isabelle, if I must ask you a second time, I will gladly do so. Will you do me the very great honor of becoming my wife?"

Tears welled in her eyes once more, but he could tell they were happy tears. She squeezed his hand tightly and nodded.

"Yes, Sandy, I will marry you. A thousand times yes!"

"Well, thank God." Sandy kissed her hand, her warm skin exciting him once more. He had her promise. She would be his and no other's.

Joyous once more, he slipped back onto the sofa next to her, her hand still in his. He was loath to give it up, as hard won as it was. They sat in companionable silence, Isabelle leaning against him, her soft scent of lilacs wafting over him. She always smelled like a bouquet of fresh flowers. He pulled her closer, resting his head atop hers. "I hope we can be in accord about our next wedding, my dear, for I wish for us to be married as soon as possible. Once you are Lady MacKay, your stepfather will have no power over you whatsoever."

"I like the sound of that very much." She wrapped her arms around him. "But I do not wish to return to London and have to face everyone who saw me flee your grandfather's house. Can we be married here, in my grandmother's house? I am certain she would love to see us married from the house my father grew up in." She twisted to look at him hopefully. "You did bring the special license with you, didn't you?"

"Of course I did." He grinned at her. "Am I not always prepared? Unfortunately," he continued solemnly, "I am not inclined to trust it now."

"What do you mean?" Isabelle sat up, concern gathering in her eyes.

"You are still only eighteen, my dear. Your parents, and more particularly your guardian, has to give his permission."

"But he already did." She cocked her head. "I was there when he signed the settlement papers."

"And I am certain your mother persuaded him to do so. It would have been too exceptional for him to try to prevent the marriage, given the station of the man you were going to wed. Now, things have changed. I have assaulted your stepfather and he may very well cite your flight from me as evidence you changed your mind and wished to break the betrothal." Sandy shook his head, regretting that satisfying punch to Grey's nose.

"My grandmother cannot act as my guardian? She is my closest relative other than my mother."

"I'm afraid not. To change a guardian would take time and money and might very well come to nothing in the end. Guardianship is almost always given to a man, particularly if they are married to the mother of the child in question.

"Then what can we do?" Isabelle's voice held a tinge of fear.

Smiling broadly, Sandy stroked her hand. "We go to Scotland. Carnwath lies less than a day's travel on the train. We can be married at the little kirk I grew up in." He sighed. "Had we been running away four years ago, we could have been married as soon as we crossed the border into Scotland—at the scandalous Gretna Green no less, and been married by the famous anvil priest."

Isabelle's eyes sparkled. "Why can't we be scandalous now,

my love?"

Sandy grinned ruefully. "Because Lord Brougham, himself married at Gretna Green years ago, passed the Marriage Act of 1856. The bill made it illegal to get married unless one of the two parties had resided in the parish in Scotland for twenty-one days. So we will have no problem if we travel all the way to Carnwath to my home parish. I have indeed resided there for much more than twenty-one days."

"I am so sorry, Sandy, to have put you to all this trouble."

"As long as you marry me, my love, it is no trouble whatsoever. I don't care how or where we do it, as long as we do it." He pointed a finger at her and wagged it in her face. "And if you even think of reneging on me again, I vow I will strum a guitar and serenade you in a loud voice under your window all night, every night, for all the world to hear."

"I said yes, I will marry you, my love." She threw her arms around him. "I will not go back on it this time."

Relief rushed through him in a wave of pure joy. He lifted her mouth to his and pressed his lips gently to hers. The sweet taste of her went straight to his head. This was what he craved, this sweetness that rushed through his veins, setting him afire with desire for her. He'd need to go slowly, more slowly than with an innocent bride. In the end, Isabelle might be more frightened about the marriage bed than she knew. She always presented a brave face, no matter what.

No matter. He was a patient man. And patience was a virtue that would be richly rewarded.

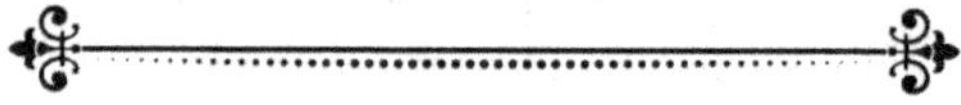

Chapter Eleven

Carnwath, Scotland
October 3

"It's like a fairytale castle!" Isabelle gasped at her first glimpse of the place where Sandy had grown up. "What's the name again?"

"Cridhe Laidir. It means 'strong heart.'"

"Cridhe Laidir." She liked the sound of the castle's name on her tongue. "You neglected to tell me it was so lovely." The pale-grey stone castle sat on a promontory that overlooked the surrounding acreage like a laird surveying his subjects. Tall spires rose at all four corners and in the middle, startling against the blue of the afternoon sky. Ivy covered some of the walls, others showed grooves made from years of water streaming down the faces.

"She's newer than most Scottish baronial castles by several hundred years. The second Baron MacKay had fought for a time in Germany, saw their castles, and insisted on bringing some of that architecture home to Scotland.

"Well, I love it." She'd be living here for most of the rest of her life. Could she be any luckier?

The late afternoon sun was beginning to set as the carriage pulled up to the door. It had been a wearying journey of almost eight hours from Carlisle to Carnwath, including two hours between trains in Glasgow. She was tired and hungry and ready for bed. The one saving grace had been her traveling gown—one of her grandmother's mourning gowns that had actually fit Isabelle fairly well. The jet-black fabric showed absolutely none of the smoke and grime from the journey, though after such strenuous traveling, Isabelle would be glad to remove it.

As the carriage stopped, Sandy had the door open and lifted Isabelle out.

"What are you doing?"

He held her in his arms as he started for the solid-looking black castle door. "Carrying you over the threshold like a good bridegroom should."

"But we aren't married yet."

"Details, details," he laughed as they approached the door.

As if by magic it opened, a tall, stately butler standing at attention just inside. "Welcome home, my lord." He bowed as Sandy carried her into the echoing stone foyer. All manner of warlike weapons hung on the walls, fierce-looking broadswords, maces, and battleaxes. A set of armor stood in each corner, polished and shiny, yet deadly.

"I had no idea the MacKays were so bloodthirsty."

"We're a small but feisty clan." Sandy set her on her feet and kissed her. "Our motto is *Gun eagal agus fior*, fearless and true."

"That certainly seems appropriate." She laughed, enchanted with the castle, both inside and out.

The butler hurried toward Sandy.

"My dear, may I present Grant, the castle's butler. Grant, Miss Isabelle Devereaux, soon to be my wife."

"Soon to be, my lord?" The butler looked confusedly from Sandy to Isabelle, then his face snapped back into its stoic lines. "I will have your bags seen to, my lord." He motioned to a nearby footman, who hurried out the door. "Will you be resting before dinner?"

"Not until after dinner, Grant. I had the coachman stop here to leave the bags and make sure dinner would be ready upon our return. We are leaving for the kirk in a few minutes' time. I insist on having our marriage solemnized before the sun goes down." He turned to gaze at Isabelle. "I will not have it said that we lived in sin, no matter for how brief a time. Come my dear." He offered Isabelle his arm. "We will be back shortly, Grant."

"Very good, my lord."

The carriage took them back down the long, tree-lined driveway, then left onto the main road toward the village of Carnwath.

"If we'd turned right, we'd be on our way to Glasgow." Sandy glanced at her and smiled. "And if we continue through the village, we'd be heading toward Edinburgh. That's a journey we'll take another time. You really must see Scotland's capital with all its rich history and landmarks. It's also the most beautiful city in the country. Some say in all the world." His eyes twinkled. "You might enjoy the shops there too."

"I suspect I would." Isabelle squeezed his arm. There would be so much to see and do and learn in her new life here with Sandy. It was an adventure she scarcely would have dreamed of two months ago.

The bright autumn foliage in the late afternoon light made the countryside appear to be aflame with brilliant red, orange, and yellow leaves as they came into the village. Thatched cottages dotted here and there gave way to a row of three pretty little houses, beyond which rose the spire of a modest-looking church.

"That's St. Mary's." Sandy nodded toward the structure. "It's been the Carnwath parish church since the thirteenth century."

"It doesn't look that old. Well, most of it doesn't." Isabelle had spied a part of the church beside the main building that seemed truly ancient.

"The main church is dated from 1799, so not very old at all." The carriage pulled up in front of an arched wooden door. "The older part there—" He nodded to his left at the smaller, badly pock-marked stone building. "—that is St. Mary's Aisle, the North transept of the original church built in 1424." He grinned as they moved toward the door. "All the small boys in the parish used to dare one another to go into it just as the sun was setting."

"You were one of those small boys, I take it?" Isabelle smiled, imagining him as a young daredevil.

"I was the ringleader." Sandy opened the door and a chill wind rushed by them.

Isabelle shivered and sped inside. The thick stone walls kept the cold in and the light out, save for the tall, narrow windows positioned at sparse intervals around the sanctuary. The light shawl her grandmother had given her this morning did little to warm her. One of the worst things about her precipitous flight north had been her lack of proper clothing, including a coat or cloak.

"Wait here and I'll go find Mr. Pettigrew, the vicar." Sandy headed toward the raised pulpit, then disappeared through the door to the side of it.

Isabelle shivered and pulled the shawl closer around her but found little warmth in it. Perhaps if she kept moving, she'd stay warmer. There were brass plaques fastened to the walls at equal distances, so she strolled over to the closest one to investigate. It was a burial plaque, commemorating Ewan and Adaira MacKay, who had died in 1622. Most likely Sandy's ancestors. She continued around the room, noting more than half the plaques belonged to MacKays.

"May I help ye?"

Isabelle jumped and whirled around.

An older gentleman, in dark clothing with a white collar, stood in the center aisle looking inquiringly at her.

Clutching her shawl, Isabelle started toward the man, obviously the vicar. "Good afternoon. Are you Mr. Pettigrew?"

"I am." He bowed his head. "Whom do I have the honor of addressing?"

"Oh, I...I'm Isabelle Devereaux." She glanced around the

sanctuary, hoping Sandy had returned. It was just her luck he was still in search of the man in front of her.

"Mrs. Devereaux?" Something in his voice sounded suspicious, although that might simply be Isabelle's notion.

"Miss Devereaux. I'm here..." Somehow it seemed wrong to announce she was here to be married when the vicar didn't know her at all.

"As I see ye are, lass." Mr. Pettigrew cocked his head, his mouth pursing. "What I'm wantin' to ken is why? Are ye here ta confess yer sins?"

"Confess...oh, no, sir. I've not committed any sin." Lord, what did the man think she'd done?

"Then ye're the first woman since the Blessed Mary herself who hasn't." Impatience in both the vicar's voice and stance made Isabelle tremble from something other than cold.

"Mr. Pettigrew, I'll thank ye no' ta terrorize th' woman who's agreed at last ta be ma wife." Sandy's voice drifted down from the upper choir loft and Isabelle breathed a sigh of relief. She cocked her head, though. That was Sandy's voice, but he was speaking differently. Suddenly, he sounded...Scottish.

"Who's that up there?" The vicar craned his head.

"Ye ken good 'n well who I am." Sandy peered over the railing.

"Aye, I ken ye now, Laird MacKay." The vicar glanced back at Isabelle. "Why did ye no' tell me who ye were, lass?"

At a loss for words, Isabelle simply shrugged. Her strength had started to flag. It had been a long day and it might be longer and stranger yet.

"I'm coming down." Sandy's voice trailed off and the muffled sound of pounding feet on a staircase followed.

"I'd had it from Lady MacKay th' lad was ta wed in London, Miss Devereaux." Mr. Pettigrew's demeanor had changed from righteous indignation to more of a conciliatory mien. "But ye'er no' married yet?"

"No, sir. We are not." Isabelle looked around, hoping Sandy

would appear before she had to say more to the vicar.

"May I ask why ye're no' wed?" Mr. Pettigrew sent Isabelle another sharp look.

The door banged open.

"Nae, ye may no' ask, Angus." Sandy hurried over to them, and Isabelle grasped his arm. Thank goodness she would not have to answer any more questions from the curious vicar. "'Tis our business alone why we came here ta marry."

Mr. Pettigrew's face fell, but he recovered himself and became quite business-like. "Very well, then, mi'lord. D'ye wish ta have th' banns read startin' this Sunday?"

For once Sandy looked sheepish. "Nae, Mr. Pettigrew. We mean ta wed this evenin'."

"This evenin'?" The vicar looked scandalized. "Ye dinna mean ta have a grand ceremony, wi' all o' th' village attendin'? I thought that might be why ye decided ta marry here."

"Nae, it's no'." Sandy shifted from one foot to the other. "But it is imperative we marry now, Mr. Pettigrew. Tonight, if ye please."

"Tonight? Ye meant it, when ye said ye needed it to be tonight?" The clergyman's countenance changed from astonishment to suspicion. "Are ye tellin' me yon lass is already in a family way, Laird MacKay? She's carryin' yer bairn?"

"No!"

"Nae!" Isabelle and Sandy spoke almost as one. They shared a look, then Sandy continued. "Miss Devereaux's family may no' wish for us ta marry."

"May no'? Tha' doesna seem ta be something ye'd be unsure o'. Either they do or they dinna." Mr. Pettigrew had grown impatient again.

"I punched her stepfather."

Mr. Pettigrew's mouth dropped open. "Go on wi' ye!"

"Sae I dinna hang about ta ask if I could still marry his daughter."

"Well, aye, in that case, I canna blame ye, lad." With a sigh,

Mr. Pettigrew turned toward the pulpit. "I'll get th' prayerbook." The vicar stopped and looked back at them. "I'll bring Mrs. Pettigrew ta be the second witness." He cocked his head. "But where's yer màthair, mi'lord?"

Sandy cut his eyes toward Isabelle, then drew in a breath. "In London, still."

Mr. Pettigrew drew himself up. "Och, an ye think I'll marry ye and have Lady MacKay cursin' me for tha rest o' me life because she wasna here ta witness it?" He shook his head until his hair fell into his eyes. "Nae, Laird MacKay. I'll no' be a party ta any such thing." The vicar turned on his heel, headed for the door.

"Och, for the love o' Christ," Sandy muttered under his breath. "Mr. Pettigrew." He raised his voice so loud, Isabelle winced. "I have ta insist ye marry us tonight or ye'll be ruining the reputation of an innocent lady."

The vicar turned, brows lowered. "'Tis ye'll be ruining the lass, mi'lord. No' I an ye canna restrain yerself 'til yer màthair returns."

"My betrothed has nowhere ta stay in Carnwath, Mr. Pettigrew, save Cridhe Laidir. Neither ma màthair nor any other lady is in residence there." Sandy stalked toward the older man so fiercely, Mr. Pettigrew started backing away. "An Miss Devereaux stays there tonight unmarried, she'll be deemed a scarlet woman when she rises in the morning, whether or no' I've touched her. That will be on yer head, vicar, no mine."

Giving Sandy a dour look, Mr. Pettigrew shook his head. "Bide a wee while I get tha prayerbook an tha witnesses." He hurried out the door, banging it loudly.

"I'm sorry you've had to endure that with Mr. Pettigrew, my love." Sandy chuckled. "He's known me all my life, and so fears my mother much more than he does me."

Waving away Mr. Pettigrew for the moment, Isabelle gazed into his face with wonder. "Sandy, how on earth did you do that?"

"Do what, my love?" He frowned, as though he truly didn't understand her question.

"Change the way you spoke to Mr. Pettigrew." Did he really not know how strange he'd sounded? "I knew you were Scottish, but you've always sounded English. I just assumed you'd grown up there."

"When I was a boy, I lived right here in Carnwath except for the summers I spent at my grandfather's estate with my Quartermain cousins." He grinned. "They're the reason why I can sound like an Englishman born and bred in the heart of London. During those early summers, I spoke with the Scottish accent I'd grown up hearing from everyone but my mother. The other boys would tease me terribly, aping my brogue until I'd run crying to Mother."

"Oh, Sandy." How cruel his cousins had been. "They were terribly mean to you."

"Well, I wasn't but a wee lad at the time. Lads are tough, don't you know. But it made me want to speak like them. So, I listened and started mimicking them. By the end of the summer, you'd have sworn I'd been raised in Hertfordshire."

"When you speak like this, I'd swear you had been." Such a remarkable talent. And she'd not known it until today.

"Of course, when I came back home, I had to return to the Scottish, else I'd have taken a drubbing from the lads in Carnwath." He shook his head. "I learned to switch from one to the other fairly easily. Good thing too. I shudder to think what would have happened to me when I went to Cambridge if I'd been speakin' ma màithair tongue."

Isabelle giggled. "You are amazing, my love."

The inner door to the sanctuary banged open and Mr. Pettigrew entered, prayerbook under his arm, followed by two ladies who looked uncommonly similar.

"Come up ta tha altar, if ye please." The vicar took his place before it, the ladies to his side. "Laird MacKay, Miss Devereaux, may I present ma wife, Mrs. Pettigrew and her sister, Mrs.

Dunnett. They've graciously agreed ta be yer witnesses."

"Thank ye, ladies. We're honored ta have ye as guests at our weddin'." Sandy bowed and Isabelle curtsied.

"Yes, thank you so much for helping make this possible for us." Isabelle was grateful for the ladies, still she hoped they could be quick about it. She was so tired by now, she thought she might begin to sway with exhaustion.

"Ahem." Mr. Pettigrew cleared his throat and Isabelle and Sandy turned to the vicar. "Are ye ready ta get on wi' it?"

"We are." Sandy took her hand and they faced the vicar.

"Very well, then. Dearly beloved, we are gathered here in the presence of God…"

CHAPTER TWELVE

BY THE TIME they arrived back at Cridhe Laidir, Isabelle was so tired she was more than happy to have Sandy carry her across the threshold once more. Once he put her down, however, her fatigue became so obvious, even to Sandy, that he suggested he order dinner to be brought to their chamber. She nodded, although she suspected she'd be too tired to even eat.

Wearily, she dragged one foot after another up the winding staircase, taking note, despite her fatigue, of the castle's rich appointments. Tapestries adorned the walls, depicting scenes of everything from a stag hunt to scenes from the Bible to fantastical animals. Interspersed with these luscious hangings were what she assumed to be family portraits in elegantly arranged groupings. The castle's magnificence helped soothe her exhausted soul.

"I sent a telegram off to my mother before we left Carlisle, informing her of our intent to marry here immediately." He grinned at her. "I daresay I shall get a somewhat less cordial one in return tomorrow. I did ask her to send my valet, Carnes, on to Scotland. And she'll have Cooper accompany her whenever she leaves Town. Until then—" He grinned and waggled his eyebrows suggestively. "—you will have to make do with me as lady's maid."

Isabelle burst out laughing. "I believe I will do just fine with only you, my dear." She sobered. "I have so few clothes, I may need little assistance at all."

"Never underestimate my mother, Isabelle. She is sending the trunks packed for our original wedding trip along with my man. And woe be to your stepfather if he tries to gainsay my mother." Sandy opened the door of their chamber, then scooped her up in his arms.

"Are you going to carry me over every threshold in the entire castle?" Isabelle was teasing, but she enjoyed the feeling of having his strong arms around her, so if he did, she wouldn't mind at all.

"I hadn't planned on it, but now you mention it…" He swung her around, making her delighted and dizzy. "I like having you in my arms, sweetheart." Slowly, he let her slide to the floor, allowing her to touch every one of his muscles. When her toes reached the floor, he grasped her head in both hands and kissed her.

Oh, but she'd come to savor those kisses. His soft lips claimed her soul, piece by piece, each time they brushed across her mouth. She hungered for them whenever they were not engaged as they now were, making her blood sizzle in her veins. Moaning softly, she slid her arms around his neck, pressing tighter against him just as he slipped his tongue into her mouth.

It had been a strange sensation the first time he'd done that, but now she craved the excitement that ensued whenever he did it. Warmth spread from the pit of her stomach down toward the deepest core of her body, more intense each time. These new, pleasurable sensations Sandy evoked in her were nothing at all like the pain and misery she'd experienced each time her stepfather had visited her bed. If she could put that monster out of her head and think only of Sandy, only of the pleasure he always brought her, perhaps she'd be ready tonight. She so wanted to be ready for him.

"Here," he said, breaking the kiss and standing back from her. "Let me unbutton you so you can get ready for bed." He nodded toward a door beside the fireplace. "They should have placed your trunk in the dressing room, which is on that side of the fireplace. On the opposite side is the necessary room."

"Necessary room?" She'd not heard of such a thing.

He grinned. "When the castle was built, they added two dressing rooms to the master's chamber. When my mother came here, she decided it was the perfect place to put a close stool and do away with the chamber pot behind a screen. She said it gave one the dignity of privacy for one's private moments. My father, who would do anything for her, moved his clothing into an adjacent room he also used as a study, and they were both very happy with the arrangement."

Isabelle began to see why Sandy was so considerate toward her. He'd had the best of examples for a perfect marriage in his parents. Pray God, they could have the same.

"I'll check on dinner and let you settle in, then we can eat and celebrate our marriage properly."

Something about those final words sent a shiver down Isabelle's spine, but she nodded and turned around. Once her bodice slackened, she started for the dressing room when his lips brushed the bare skin at the nape of her neck. The kiss was so unexpected, so…sensual, she almost cried out. And suddenly, apprehension replaced fatigue. Tonight was their wedding night and Isabelle knew what that must mean.

"I'll be back shortly, sweetheart." Sandy dropped another kiss on her neck, making her tremble, then left.

Isabelle hurried to the dressing room, lit a lamp—although it took her shaking hands three tries to light a match—and hastily readied herself for bed. She dug through the trunk and pulled out the only nightgown she had—an old-fashioned one from her grandmother with a high collar and long sleeves, scratchy lace at collar and cuffs. Well, the garment certainly wasn't meant to arouse anyone. Perhaps her husband wouldn't wish to pursue amorous congress at all after he saw her in that. With a sigh, Isabelle pulled it over her head and padded back out into the bedchamber.

Half the room was taken up with a huge four-poster bed with

blue and gold damasked covers and curtains. It dwarfed everything else in the room, none of which she'd noted when they'd first entered it. She'd been too swept up in the moment with Sandy to pay attention to anything else.

Now, as she walked to the massive bed, she noted the chaise drawn up before the fireplace, the cherry secretary desk in the corner, and a small table and chairs before the drawn drapes over the window. She liked the stately room, with its excellent appointments. It was a trifle masculine, but if Sandy allowed it, she could add some feminine touches, like a toilette table.

He'd be back soon. Isabelle rubbed her hands against her arms, trying to subdue the chill that suddenly shook her. Where should she be when he returned? Either on the chaise before the fire or in the bed waiting were the obvious choices. Perhaps she should just go ahead and crawl into bed. She doubted she'd eat any dinner with the way her stomach was roiling anyway.

The enormous four-poster loomed even larger as she mounted the stepstool. The bed would easily accommodate at least four people. Of course, it would only need to sleep two tonight. Not that Isabelle expected sleep would be the primary concern.

Hastily she crawled beneath the covers, pulled them up to her chin, and awaited her bridegroom.

"ISABELLE."

Someone was shaking her shoulder, but she was so warm and cozy, she didn't want to wake up.

"Isabelle, wake up, love."

The unexpected endearment startled her enough to open her eyes. She was in the master bedchamber at Cridhe Laidir. And she was married to… "Sandy?"

"I'm here, love."

She poked her head up. "I'm sorry I fell asleep but—"

And there he stood, barefoot before the fireplace, wearing only his shirt and breeches and sporting a wicked grin. "I'm almost through, my dear."

Lord, never had she seen a man in such a state of undress. Her eyes widened as he pulled his braces down and tugged his shirt out of his pants so it fell almost to his knees. "Do you want any dinner? It's there on the table. I'd be happy to serve you."

She glanced at plates of chicken and vegetables and shook her head. Food was the last thing she wanted at the moment. "I'm not hungry."

"I wasn't either, although I did have some wine to fortify me. Would you like some?"

The idea of wine sounded good, but again she shook her head.

"Perhaps later, then." With a practiced hand, he stripped his trousers off and tossed them onto the pile of clothes under the table. "There, that's better."

Isabelle wasn't certain she agreed with that. His lack of clothing gave him almost an animal quality as he stalked toward the bed. His shirt flowing around him showed off his legs from knees to feet. She'd never seen a man's legs before, though somehow, she hadn't expected them to be hairy. Sandy's were well-muscled, with a shapely calf, but definitely hairy. Was the rest of his body like that?

Her cheeks flamed as though she'd stepped into the mid-day sun. She'd find out soon enough, too, for her husband was almost upon her. To avoid seeing anything else, she stared straight ahead at a painting of a group of hunters cornering a stag.

Oh, but she wasn't prepared for this at all. She needed more time to get used to the idea of sharing intimacies with Sandy, although all the time in the world might not help her with that. No, it would be all right. She had survived before, she could do so again.

"Would you like me to blow out the lamp?"

Isabelle jumped at the voice so close beside her. "Oh, yes,

please blow it out." She didn't want to see anything at all if she could help it.

A moment later, they were plunged into darkness and Isabelle squealed. The bed dipped as Sandy slid beneath the covers next to her.

"Don't be frightened, love." His silky voice made her shiver.

But this was Sandy, the man she knew and loved. The one she trusted. He was right. There was nothing to be frightened of.

"Lay down, sweetheart."

She hadn't realized she was still sitting up in the bed. Awkwardly, she slid down, inch by inch, until her head rested on the pillow. Stiff as a tree trunk, nonetheless, she was lying down.

"May I kiss the bride?"

Isabelle jumped. When had he gotten so close? Now his lips were against her ear, his breath tickling her skin, heating her whole body with just his voice. There was nothing wrong with this…closeness. Nor with a kiss. She'd kissed Sandy many times before. Nothing to be frightened of at all.

Turning toward him, she sensed his mouth close to hers, then his lips covered hers, pressing firmly. She needed to relax, to not think about every movement he was making. Instead, she needed to let go, abandon herself to the moment and simply kiss him.

On impulse, she slid her arm over his shoulder, wanting to bring him closer—and met the bare skin of his back. Isabelle froze. When had he taken off his shirt? That could only mean that he was naked all the way down and lying next to her.

Heart beating so fast she could scarcely breathe, Isabelle tried to inch away from him, but as she did, she managed to bring him with her, until she lay flat on her back, with Sandy lying on top of her. Lying naked on top of her.

Paralyzed beneath a man…just like before. Eyes shut tight, unable to speak, Isabelle tried to will him away. That would never work, but what else could she do? He shifted, the hardened part of him pressing against her thighs. Trembling, she waited for him to—

"Isabelle?"

Her eyes flew open, though in the darkness she couldn't see anything. She knew his voice, nonetheless. The man she loved. The man she trusted. "Yes."

He raised himself off her. "Am I hurting you, my love?"

She shook her head, but of course, he couldn't see that. "No, you're not hurting me." She tried to make her voice sound confident, but it didn't.

"Would you rather I stop right now?"

Torn by indecision, Isabelle couldn't speak at first. One tiny part of her didn't want him to stop. She wished to be a good wife to Sandy in every way. If he just got on with it now, she could get through it, in the hope the next time would be better. Fighting to keep the tremor out of her voice, she kept the answer as short as possible. "No."

The touch of his finger stroking her cheek made her flinch.

"You don't have to lie to me, sweetheart."

The gentleness in his voice smote her heart. He was too good to her. "I'm not lying."

"Your words may say one thing, my dear, but your body is telling me a different story. I know when a woman is willing, eager even. And I know when she is not." His lips brushed her forehead and suddenly his weight lifted from her. "If you are not ready for these intimacies with me, we can wait. We have all the time in the world. I'm a patient man."

In those last words, she heard a smile.

The bed creaked as he lay back on his side of the bed.

For the briefest of moments, she wanted to call him back, wanted to feel his weight on her again, feel his warmth close to her. But he was right. When he was on top of her, she hadn't wanted that weight and everything it implied. Yet she wanted Sandy, with all her heart.

But only a little bit of him for now.

As though he'd read her thoughts, he clasped her hand in his, the warmth of his skin comforting beyond belief.

"Better?"

"Much better." Twisting quickly, she placed a light kiss on his bare shoulder. Truly this man possessed the proverbial patience of a saint. If she looked closely, she might see the faint light of a halo around his head. Not many men would agree to spend their wedding night holding hands with their frightened bride. Isabelle gave his hand a squeeze. Somehow she would overcome this fear, and as soon as she possibly could.

She didn't wish to try Sandy for too long—even a saint's control could be broken if unrelentingly tested. If she set her mind to it, it shouldn't take her long to convince herself she could enjoy intimacy with her husband. As Sandy had said, they had time.

By the grace of God, they wouldn't need much.

CHAPTER THIRTEEN

BRILLIANT AUTUMN SUNLIGHT streaming across the bed woke Sandy next morning. He blinked sleepily and turned over to be confronted with the endearing sight of his wife, turned toward him, one hand cupping her cheek, her raven hair tousled over the pillow down onto her shoulder. It was a sight he'd enjoy waking up to for the rest of his life.

Sighing, he lay back on his pillow, the pleasant dream he'd awakened from of making love to his wife under an apple tree of all things was fading, although the residue of the erotic encounter could be seen in his rather painful erection. Likely also the result of his unsuccessful wedding night. He'd suspected they would need to spend more time together before Isabelle was ready to experience the true pleasures of the marriage bed, but that didn't mean his own need was any less immediate. With a final look at his peacefully sleeping bride, Sandy slid out of bed and padded over to the door to the necessary. He didn't want to disturb Isabelle when he could take care of this matter privately.

When he returned, a great deal more relaxed, he noted their uneaten dinner had been taken away by the servants, likely when they'd opened the drapes. He rang the bell, then headed to the dressing room and donned his gold and black silk dressing gown. Glancing in the room's full-length mirror, Sandy grabbed a comb and ran it through his hair. It wouldn't do for Isabelle to see him so disheveled. He hurried out just as the door opened, and the footman entered. "Yes, mi'lord?"

"Bring breakfast as soon as possible, George. I'm not certain what Lady MacKay requires, but for now, ask Cook to prepare tea and chocolate, some bannocks, eggs, sausage, and tattie scones. I think that will do us."

"Yes, mi'lord." George bowed and retreated.

Stretching, Sandy sauntered over to the bed, hopped up on it, then stretched out on top of the covers. Propping himself up on one hand, he settled in to watch his wife sleep. A lock of hair had fallen over her face and he reached out to move it out of the way. As he did so, her eyes fluttered open, grew round in fear, the irises a startling blue against the whites, then recognition hit and she relaxed again. "Good morning, husband."

"Good morning, wife." Even sleep tousled and apprehensive, she was the most beautiful woman he'd ever seen. Once she came to trust him not to hurt her, as that brute had done, they would have a wonderful life together. "I've just ordered our breakfast served here, so if you need to visit the necessary, you have some time."

Her cheeks pinkened, but she nodded and slithered out of the bed. Her feet made a thump as she hit the floor, then she hurried to the door on the right of the fireplace and disappeared from view.

Sandy lay back on the bed, hand over his head, fully aware that even the sight of Isabelle swathed in voluminous white linen and lace had aroused him so thoroughly, he might have to repeat his actions from earlier to get relief. That or upend the washing water over his head. And he had to admit that even cold water might not work to quench his ardor. Something about Isabelle simply made his hunger for her soar. Well, they'd never get through breakfast if he didn't remedy his desire. Perhaps out of sight, out of mind. He hopped up off the bed and sped to the dressing room. After rummaging around for a moment, he pulled out the item he sought and went back to the bedroom.

Isabelle had returned and stood gazing about. "I wondered where you'd gone."

"I thought we could eat at the table and you'd feel better with a dressing gown. Since you don't have one of your own here yet, perhaps you'd like to use one of mine." He opened the grey silk jacquard banyan and held it out for her. Sandy had grown tired of it several years ago, but hadn't disposed of it yet. Now it could be put to good use.

"Oh, thank you, Sandy." She immediately backed toward him, her *derriere* swaying temptingly as she walked backward with care.

Sandy gulped but held the dressing gown out for her until her arms slid into it. She wrapped it around her, tying the belt with a flourish.

"How do I look?" Stretching her arms out, she smiled charmingly as she spun around.

With more than a little difficulty, Sandy bit back a groan of pure lust. "As beautiful as always my dear." He led her quickly to the table and pulled out her chair. If she was hidden by the table, it might help a little. At least it would conceal his erection.

"Do you have something in mind to do today, my lord?"

If only she knew the true answer to that question, she wouldn't be sitting there so calmly. Sandy shook that thought out of his head before answering. "As soon as breakfast is done, we will dress and vacate the bedchamber so the footmen can begin emptying my things out of the dressing room and putting them into the study. My father had shelves and hooks and a wardrobe or two installed for his clothing. Mine will fit there just as well. Then, I'm hoping Carnes and your luggage arrive before noon. While he is seeing to arranging my things, you can unpack to your heart's content."

"It does sound like a busy day." She sighed. "I had hoped to spend some time with you. We are still getting to know one another."

True, but he couldn't control himself around her all twenty-four hours of the day. "And we will spend time together, love. We will have breakfast." What else might be safe to spend time with her doing? "Then luncheon. And tonight, we will have a sumptuous dinner in the formal dining room again. I'll instruct Cook to make it an occasion, with all her best dishes." By then, they might be too full to think of amorous congress. Not that he'd ever been that full in his life. "You'll enjoy it."

"I want to enjoy time with you in other ways than just dining, Sandy. Can you think of something else we can do together?"

As Sandy stared at her, he could tell the exact moment she realized what she had just said.

Isabelle went red from the top of her cleavage to the tips of her petite ears. No telling what else might have turned red had breakfast not arrived.

The footman carried in the laden tray, set it on the bed and began to lay the table. In the process of setting the dishes, Isabelle's embarrassment appeared to have subsided and she dug into the eggs and bacon, seeming to enjoy the bannocks particularly.

He helped himself to eggs and bannocks and the tattie scones, a favorite since he was a boy. Of course, there were many things he and Isabelle could do together that did not involve food in the least. Things he'd love to show her, but which would likely not be appreciated at this juncture. He'd give her another day to settle in and tonight they could try again to consummate their marriage.

If this slow approach to her apprehensions didn't bear fruit soon, he'd be forced to renege on his marriage vows and go off to live like a monk. St. Paul had it right. It was better to marry than to burn. But as Paul likely never had a wife, he might not be the best authority on that advice. Especially not when being married was making him burn with passion all the hotter.

"YOU MUST GIVE my compliments to Cook, Sandy. The woman has fed us gloriously and steadily throughout the entire day." Isabelle preceded her husband into their bedchamber, scarcely able to climb the stairs after the delicious dinner of beef and veal, kidney pie, chicken in white wine sauce, and an untold number of side dishes and savories. She might have to resort to Grandmama's nightgown again tonight if the tightness of her corset was any indication.

Making a beeline for the bed, Isabelle thought of one thing alone—sleep. She toppled onto the tall mattress, face first into the soft covers, feet still flat on the floor—a comfortable enough position that she might just fall asleep here and now. She sighed contentedly.

Her bliss was interrupted by the sudden sensation of someone leaning over her, pressing against her hoops. Then her husband's voice whispered in her ear, "These clothes can't be comfortable. Would you like me to help you out of them?"

All thoughts of sleep flew out of her head as that sensual voice filled it instead. "Yes, that would be wonderful, Sandy."

He slipped his hands under her breasts and lifted her until she stood so her back pressed against his chest. He slid his lips down the length of her neck, scattering tiny kisses as he went. The hairs on her arms rose straight up as she quivered and moaned. His mouth on her skin made her forget everything except the delicious shivers that raced down her spine.

Slowly, gently, he slipped his hands up over her breasts, cupping them, squeezing them, making them ache with a longing she didn't understand. Even through all the layers of her clothing, she could feel his fingers stroking her nipples. Her moans increased.

"More?" he whispered.

"Oh, yes." Voice low and breathy, she wasn't sure what that more would be, only that she wanted it without question.

Nimble fingers unbuttoned the bodice of her gown, laying open to view her corset and corset cover. Sandy slipped his hands into it and pulled gently until her breasts popped free, sitting atop the edge of her corset, completely exposed to his avid gaze.

Not knowing where to look, Isabelle closed her eyes, then gasped as he stroked her breasts, circling the nipples until they hardened and ached. Breathing faster, she leaned back against Sandy's hard chest, straining into his hands as he teased and fondled her aching flesh.

Deep down in her core, a fire came to life—a peculiar sensation she'd never felt before that began to grow inside her, making her want his hands all over her naked body.

"Do you like that, my love?" Sandy continued stroking the tips of her nipples, each stroke plucking a chord deep within her.

"Yes, yes." Moans deepening, Isabelle writhed against him. She'd never dreamed his touch could feel so wonderful.

Then his lips descended her neck again, kisses light as errant thistledown, his tongue gliding over the surface of her skin. He turned her slightly toward him until his tongue touched the very tip of her nipple.

Isabelle shuddered, her knees going weak. The ache at her core grew stronger, and she twisted against him, caught up in a frenzy she couldn't fathom. "What…what…"

"Shhh…"

She couldn't speak, could scarcely breathe.

Without warning, he engulfed her nipple.

Isabelle's breath stopped.

Sandy sucked on her breast, laving her nipple, then ever so gently scraping it with his teeth.

The ache in Isabelle's core exploded. She gasped as she shattered deep within herself, strained back against Sandy, and knew no more.

WHEN HER EYES fluttered open, Isabelle lay in the huge four-poster bed looking up at a canopy of dark blue damask, underneath the matching coverlet. Naked.

Sandy sat on the side of the bed, his worried face clearing. "Are you feeling better?"

Isabelle frowned. "What happened?"

"We had begun to make love and you fainted."

Heat spiked in her cheeks as the image of his mouth on her breasts came back to her. She recalled that growing ache at her core, then the utterly rapturous release, but nothing else.

"Can you tell me what happened?" That apprehensive look had returned. "Did I do something to hurt you?"

"No, no, my love." Shaking her head vehemently, she sat up and grasped his hand. "You were kissing me…kissing my…" She couldn't say it, not while she was looking at him. Turning her head, she whispered, "My breasts." Would he know what had happened to her? Why her core had ached, but not with a pain she could describe? "I felt so strange inside. Just here." She laid her hand on her abdomen. "But deep inside." Isabelle frowned. "It didn't hurt, exactly, but it grew and grew until you—" She looked away again, unable to meet his darkening eyes. "—did…that last thing… it was like something burst inside me all of a sudden."

"Did it hurt when you felt this 'bursting' sensation?" Sandy's voice sounded peculiar, as though he wanted to laugh.

But he wouldn't laugh at her, would he? Not if something was wrong with her. "No, it didn't hurt." She risked a look at him, to find he *was* smiling. "It was the greatest pleasure I've ever felt." Which made no sense. She frowned. "But you say I fainted. One does not faint from pleasure."

Gently, Sandy cupped her cheek, his eyes a darker blue than she'd ever seen them. "Apparently some people do, my love. I've heard of this happening, but not to me or to anyone I have ever known. It's called 'la petite mort.'"

"The little death?" Isabelle pulled the covers up close to her chin. This didn't sound good at all. "I didn't really die, did I?"

"No, sweetheart." He smiled at her, and the strange feeling

down below flared up again. "But it does mean you experienced extreme pleasure when I was tasting your breasts." He peered intently at her. "You said you liked it, didn't you? It didn't hurt or frighten you?"

"No, not at all." Staring into his eyes, she could feel her core begin to spiral again. "I…I did like it."

"I did too." He rose from the bed and with one fluid movement, pulled his jacket off, revealing glimpses of a well-muscled chest through his unbuttoned shirt. "Would you like me to do it again?"

Startled by the sight of her practically naked husband, Isabelle had to tear her gaze away from the fascinating play of his muscles as he bent to remove his shoes, in order to take in his question.

"You want to do it again?" She'd started getting very warm under the covers.

"We can do anything we want, love. As long as you wish it." His nimble fingers were now making short work of the buttons of his fly fall. When his trousers dropped to the floor, Isabelle gasped to discover one part of him, while still invisible to her eyes, was making itself known by tenting his shirt.

Pulse quickening, Isabelle couldn't tear her gaze from him as he stalked toward the bed.

"May I join you, my lady?"

Breath coming quicker, Isabelle nodded. The tension building within her wasn't frighting but thrilling.

Her husband lifted the covers and crawled in beside her. Turning on his side to face her, he propped his head on one hand. With the other, he ran his finger down her cheek. "You must promise me that if you are frightened or uncomfortable with anything we do, you will tell me to stop."

"I'm not frightened." She needed to assure him of that. "But I promise." And she would, however having experienced that incredible feeling of release, she was eager for him to show her more. Trying to play the coquette, she gazed pointedly at his chest. "Are you going to play fair, my lord?" She then peeped under the covers at her own nakedness. "You have the advantage as I see it."

"You are bold, lady." Laughing, he sat up in the bed. "But I will comply and put us on even footing." He pulled his shirt up and over his head, then flung the garment into the center of the room where it floated down to land in the middle of the carpet. Twisting toward her, he held his arms outstretched to either side. "Look your fill, madam."

Eagerly, Isabelle did just that, drinking in the sleek, well-muscled arms, broad shoulders and chest, the latter with a furry mat of dark hair all over it. She ran a finger down to his stomach, the fine hairs parting before her. Something about Sandy's carefree demeanor made her bold—not bold enough, however, to continue her trek beneath the covers that hid the rest of his body.

"Now, fair is fair." He stared hungrily at her. "May I look once more at your beauty—unadorned?"

Heat tinged her cheeks. He'd obviously seen her unclothed when he had been the one to unclothe her. And he had displayed himself for her pleasure. Apparently married women were supposed to be bolder when with their husbands. Quickly, before she could talk herself out of it, Isabelle sat up, throwing off the covers as she did so.

The room's cooler air made her flesh prickle, her nipples drawing into themselves like two hard, dark points in a pale sea. Deliberately, she turned toward Sandy, to find him staring hard at her breasts. When he licked his lips, she could almost feel his tongue on her skin, and her core throbbed.

Slowly, Sandy leaned forward until his lips fastened on her neck.

Isabelle sucked in a breath, then moaned aloud as he laved her skin with his tongue. Little by little, he strayed downward, taking his time, making her anticipate each kiss. As he descended, so did she, leaning back until her head sank onto the pillow, his mouth poised above her nipple.

Holding her breath, she stared at him as he licked the tip, then blew gently across it. The slight chill hardened her flesh again and sent a surge of heat down to her core. She grasped the headboard and braced herself.

"Does that feel good?" Sandy's head moved to the other breast, the hot air of his breath setting her on fire.

"Yes, Sandy, yes—oh!" He'd taken her whole nipple into his mouth. She writhed with the sheer pleasure of it. Never had anything felt so good before. "Oh, Sandy, oh yes." He sucked harder and she thought she'd go mad from the rapture of the moment.

Then he skimmed his hand over her stomach, down over her belly, toward that place…

Isabelle froze, her pleasure evaporating like water in the sunlight. She lay stiff, unmoving, waiting in dread for him to continue down…there.

He snatched his hand back and sat up. "You were supposed to tell me to stop, Isabelle."

She opened her eyes—though she didn't remember closing them—to stare into Sandy's concerned face hovering over her. "I will."

"But you didn't."

She had wanted to say something, but it wasn't fair to her husband. He'd been so patient with her last night. He shouldn't have to wait forever. "You can go on with…what you were doing. I'll be fine."

"No, you will not." He stared so hard at her, she tried to shrink back into the pillow. "I can tell if a woman is enjoying herself in bed, just as you were when I was fondling your breasts. But when I started to do other things, you stopped having any pleasure in it at all." Sandy shook his head. "That will not do at all, Isabelle. You have born enough. I will not add to that burden."

He was such a good man. She couldn't allow him to continue to sacrifice his own needs for her. "I must submit to it sometime,

Sandy. It's not fair to you." Struggling to sit up, she managed to pull herself to where she could lean her back against the massive carved headboard. "I know you wish to do…more."

"I wish to make love to my wife, yes." He cupped her cheek, his touch soothing and gentle. "Very much so, my love. However, I will get no pleasure from an act that frightens you or from which you will receive no pleasure."

Isabelle pressed his hand against her cheek. "Let us try again. I just have to…become used to you and what husbands and wives do." Despite her coaxing, his face remained firm. "Please, Sandy?"

For a moment, she believed she had convinced him, because he seemed to be weighing something in the balance. Then, with a deep sigh, he shook his head. "I am afraid not, my love. Much as it pains me, at this moment I do not trust you to stop me, nor do I truly trust me to stop myself."

He flung off the covers revealing his member, fully aroused and ready to complete its marital duty. "Some men can control themselves better than others, and I always fancied myself one of them. However, I have never been tempted by anyone as bewitching as you." He climbed down off the bed, stalked over to the center of the room and Isabelle was treated to a magnificent sight of his round, firm buttocks as he bent to retrieve his shirt. Snaking it over his head, he shrugged it into place, his cock again tenting the garment. "I do not wish for you to tell me to stop, and I be unable to do so."

"But where will you go, Sandy?" Miserable now that he had abandoned her bed, Isabelle struggled not to cry. She didn't want to make either of them feel worse.

"The castle sports around twenty-five bedrooms, my love." He paused at the door, stiffly pulling on his trousers. "I intend to find one where I can take a cold bath."

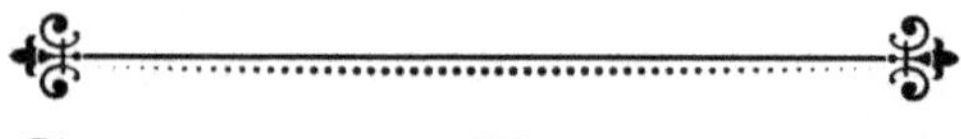

Chapter Fourteen

Next morning, Isabelle awakened early, despite a restless night's sleep. She'd been lonely in the big bed by herself, although she didn't blame Sandy at all for leaving her. There was no reason for him to stay and be tempted all night. He'd sounded as though he'd been in pain when he'd left, which was likely her fault. Hopefully, that would not happen again.

Missing Cooper's help terribly, she still managed to dress herself in one of the gowns that had arrived yesterday—a fresh deep blue and cream stripe with ruffles at the hem and edges of the wide belle sleeves. It made her happy to have her own clothes to wear once more. Fortunately, it fastened in the front, as did her stays, so she'd managed without help of either a maid or her husband, although she'd certainly have welcomed the latter. After twisting her hair up in a simple chignon, she fastened cameo earrings in her ears and a matching necklace around her neck, now ready to face the world.

Once outside the bedchamber, she looked about for a footman to direct her to the breakfast room, but the corridor was empty. Well, she'd just have to find her own way. Wandering down the hall, Isabelle enjoyed the various paintings on the walls, although she didn't recognize any of them from yesterday's trek upstairs. She was coming to a crossroads. Perhaps something would be familiar there.

A staircase led downward, and Isabelle took it gratefully, although she was certain it wasn't the main staircase she'd come up yesterday. As the stairs curved around, Isabelle restrained herself from calling out, even though she was beginning to believe herself the single living soul in the castle. She arrived at the ground floor, where finally she saw bustling activity.

The stairs gave onto the kitchen, where the cook and maids were busy filling serving pans with delicious smelling food. A maid rushed by with a pan of sausages and Isabelle's mouth watered. She'd best speak up or she might starve in the midst of all this bounty. "Pardon me."

A maid carrying a tray of toast screamed and jumped, sending toast flying every which way. "I beg pardon, miss." She bent to retrieve the scattered bread. Looking up at Isabelle again, the girl shot to her feet and curtsied. "Beg pardon, m'lady. You're the new Lady MacKay, aren't you?"

"I am." Smiling, Isabelle's trepidations melted away. At least she wasn't the only person in the castle who didn't know what to do. "And you are?"

"Morag, m'lady." She curtsied again, looking like a cornered rabbit. "I'm sorry about the toast."

"Please don't worry about it. If you want, I'll speak to Cook and let her know it was my fault." Isabelle looked around. They were in a corridor that likely led from the kitchen to the stairs that went up to the first floor and the dining rooms. "But more important, can you show me the way to the breakfast room? I'm afraid I'm completely lost."

"Oh, yes, m'lady." Morag finished collecting the scattered toast in her apron, then led Isabelle over to a small set of stairs. "Up these steps, then turn to the left and that's the breakfast room. I don't think Lord MacKay is there yet. He wasn't a few minutes ago when I set the parritch out."

"Thank you, Morag. You've been so much help to me. I'll be certain to talk to Cook." Isabelle didn't want the young girl to be scolded, or worse, sacked, for a small infraction that was Isabelle's fault alone. She mounted the steps, feeling somehow more confident than she had since arriving at Cridhe Laidir.

The breakfast room was empty, save for the sideboard already groaning with silver dishes that smelled heavenly. Isabelle seated herself at one end of the table, unsure if she should serve herself or wait for a footman to appear to serve her. At least, after today, she'd know what to expect.

Just like tonight. Once she and Sandy lay together as husband and wife, she'd know what it would be like, what he would do and how he would do it. She loved that Sandy was so thoughtful and caring about her feelings, but he also needed to allow her to get through this very difficult...activity by allowing her to get through it.

Isabelle had just laid her napkin in her lap when Sandy appeared in the doorway looking rather disturbed.

"There you are." His puckered countenance smoothed out. "I've been looking for you."

"Did you think you'd lost me?" She smiled, hoping to strike the exact correct teasing tone.

"That has actually been known to happen here." Sandy came over and kissed her forehead. "When we tour the house, we can look for their bones."

"Sandy!" He could be such a tease himself.

"Would you like me to make you a plate?"

"Yes, please. You should know I don't like fish and I don't care much for oatmeal." The thick, unappetizing paste had never appealed to her. "And you should also know that there's no toast. At least, not at the moment, due to an unfortunate accident."

Her husband turned away from the food to look at her, one eyebrow cocked high. "Am I to assume you had something to do with the lack of toast at the table?"

"You may." Isabelle grinned at him. "I ended up in the kitchen after I left the bedchamber and startled one of the kitchen maids." She giggled. "Toast flew everywhere."

"I am certain Mrs. Fletcher is remedying that this very moment. She knows the depth of my affinity for well-toasted bread." Carrying two heavily laden plates with ease, Sandy set the one with a little less food in front of her then, instead of heading for the far end of the table, he set his platter in front of the chair to her immediate left and plopped down in it. "I always thought it odd that my parents ate with so much space in between them. I resolved early on that unless there were more than a handful of guests, I would not stand on ceremony at meals, but would allow people to seat themselves where they wished."

Isabelle nodded as she attempted to find the best way to attack the mountain of food before her. "I think that is sensible. If we don't have anyone else taking up space at the table, it will be horridly difficult to hold any sort of conversation at all." She glanced at her husband, who was tucking in with gusto. "Like this morning. We can converse so much better when we are close to one another."

His mouth full of kippers and bacon, Sandy nodded.

"And I think we must converse on a very important matter." She stared him straight in the eyes. "Last night."

Sandy's brows rose, but he nodded and carefully swallowed. "Yes, I suppose we must."

"I want to propose that we try again tonight." Isabelle touched his hand, resting beside his plate. "I am so very grateful for your solicitous behavior last evening. I have said it before and I'll continue to do so, that you are an angel or a saint with the patience you've shown me. You should use your halo to light you to bed, my dear. But, the first time for anything is always difficult. This will be our first time together as husband and wife. Once we are through that, we will know what to expect." She dropped her gaze. "And if, like last night, I am frightened, or upset, I promise to let you know."

"You are correct, my love." He laid down his knife and fork and took her hand. "We must move past this 'first' time. And the only way to do that is to simply keep moving forward." He squeezed her hand. "Very well. Today we will tour the house and we will have luncheon together. This afternoon I must attend to some business and you may begin to familiarize yourself with the running of the house."

"Oh, but your mother—"

"I am not certain how active she will wish to continue to be with the day-to-day running of the house. She may, in fact, wish to remove herself to the dowager house so that we may find our own way." He chuckled. "So many questions to be answered so quickly. Still, I will leave you the afternoon to arrange your schedule to your liking. Then tonight after dinner..." he leaned toward her and whispered, "we will engage in sexual congress to our hearts' content."

"Sandy!" She couldn't help but laugh, which might have been his purpose all along.

"However," he said, sitting back in his chair, his demeanor becoming serious once more, "you had best keep your word about telling me if you are frightened or wish for me to stop. If you do not, I will not be adverse to turning you over my knee and spanking you if you misbehave."

Isabelle gasped and laughed, until she realized he was serious. "Sandy, you wouldn't!"

"Do you wish to test me and find out?" He cocked his head, waiting.

"No," she replied hastily. That no-nonsense look in his eyes told her that was one test she did not want to fail. He truly cared about her well-being, which was special in its own way. No other man, save her father, had ever cared so much about her and how she felt about things. By some miracle, she'd stumbled upon another such man. And with the grace of God, she would find a way to hold tight to him.

THE DAY HAD flown by much faster than Isabelle would have

believed it. She and Sandy had spent much of the morning together, going over the house, talking about changes or needed repairs to the castle. Isabelle had had no idea it took so much work to keep up a castle that seemed overrun by servants. Yet there was going to be much work for them to do to keep Cridhe Laidir running smoothly. The afternoon she'd spent writing to her mother, then tore the letter up, unsure if she should reveal her whereabouts to Ambrose. Afterward she'd remembered Lady MacKay had sent her trunks with Sandy's valet, so both her mother and stepfather would likely know her location. Not that it mattered. She was married to Sandy, Lord MacKay. Indeed, she was Lady MacKay. Ambrose could no longer hurt her.

Now she sat at her toilette table, rubbing lotion into her hands, waiting for Sandy with much excitement and a little trepidation. As long as her excitement outweighed everything else, she'd be fine. It was comforting to have her own clothes and things around her, even though many were new, like the nightgown and robe set she was wearing of pleated white cotton with an applique of white flowers and vines along the front opening and around the bottom hem. It was a beautiful garment that warmed her inside and out. However, she intended to wear it as little as possible tonight. Her cheeks heated at that thought, but it was nothing but the truth. She shot a glance at the door. Perhaps she should begin without the gown at all.

Scandalous thought, except she *was* married. Married people should be able to do what they wanted in the privacy of their own bedchamber. Without pausing, afraid she'd change her mind, she stood, shed the robe, then grabbed the hem of the gown and pulled it over her head. The room was much chillier without her clothing. The hairs all over her body pricked up and her nipples hardened. She hadn't realized she'd be so cold.

Padding over to the dressing room, she had to quicken her pace before she started shivering. She grabbed the white and gold silk shawl her grandmother had given her and slung it around her shoulders. Better. The shawl was long enough to cover a good amount of skin, but still leave enough of her exposed to pique her husband's interest. She returned to the chair, draped the garment more provocatively around her, then set back to await Sandy.

About the time she was contemplating stirring up the fire to warm her more, the door opened.

Isabelle arched her back—thrusting her breasts out even more—and smiled broadly.

Sandy took one step over the threshold and stopped dead at the sight of her. His eyes grew large, the pupils darkening to jet.

"Good evening, my lord." Oh, but she hoped it would be.

"Good evening." His words came out low, almost guttural, as though he could scarcely speak. He pushed the door shut with a bang, continuing to stare at her, the look of hunger growing on his face.

Uncertain what to do next in this impromptu seduction of her husband, Isabelle rose, pulling the shawl around her so she was mostly covered, and sauntered toward the four-poster. She gave him what she hoped was a sultry look over her shoulder and said, "Will you come to bed?"

In two steps Sandy reached her, grabbed her to him and sank his mouth down onto hers. The suddenness of his movement took her breath away. She clung to him, letting him drink her in as she did him. Slipping her arms around his neck, Isabelle kissed him back, thrust her tongue into his mouth, unexpectedly wanting to possess him with a ferocity she'd never known before.

Scooping her into his arms, he then strode the few remaining steps to the looming bed. He broke the kiss to set her down on the mattress, then tore off his jacket and shirt and ripped the buttons from his fall.

Amazed at the speed with which her husband disrobed, Isabelle gazed at him, her hunger growing as bit by bit, his body came into view. He kicked off his shoes, and snaked the trousers down his legs, revealing his cock once again willing and eager. His clothing dispensed with, Sandy gathered her into his arms, pulling her fully against his naked body. The incredible warmth of his skin seemed to soak into her immediately, creating a fire within—a fire she wanted to stoke until the house burned down.

He peered into her face, his countenance sober. "You remember the rules, don't you, Isabelle?"

She nodded. She'd thought about little else all day. "If I am frightened in any way, I will tell you to stop."

"Or if I hurt you."

She cupped his dear face. "You would never do that, Sandy. But I will tell you."

"Very well." He slid her back into the middle of the bed then climbed up beside her. "Where were we last night? Ah, yes. I was here."

As he lowered his head to her breast, Isabelle couldn't control her trembling. It wasn't fear—far from it. The anticipation of having his mouth on her drove her into a frenzy, until he engulfed her breast in his mouth and she moaned loudly. Each stroke of his tongue stoked the fire deep inside her. Her moaning increased as her core began to coil like before. Yes, this was what she wanted.

His hand strayed downward, brushed the soft curls at the apex of her thighs and she froze once more, but immediately shook her head. "No, don't stop." She grasped his hand to keep it there. "Please."

"Very well." He continued to stroke her, back and forth, at the same time laving and sucking her breasts.

Never had she felt anything so intensely pleasurable. And it was pleasurable. She had nothing to fear from Sandy.

He moved his hand to her thigh. "Will you open for me, love?"

Focusing on the arousing sensations and nothing else, Isabelle kept her gaze on him and did as he asked.

First tentatively, then with more assurance, Sandy moved his hand between her legs and stroked upward.

The coiling at her core soared, her hips rising off the bed as she writhed against him and cried out. He tried to remove his hand, but she shook her head violently. "No, please, don't stop."

Sandy grunted, but redoubled his efforts, his fingers continuing to play, tracing her folds, stroking the strange wetness that suddenly appeared, making her core continue to throb. Then he touched a spot that made her gasp and moan with pleasure.

"Was that a stop?" he whispered, although he continued to stroke that incredibly sensitive spot.

"No, no, it wasn't. Oh, Sandy..." She twisted the sheets in her hands, tossing back and forth, wanting to fly to pieces as she had before, but she couldn't quite reach that peak. "It feels so good, but somehow, it's not...enough."

He kissed her neck fiercely and slid behind her. "Lift your leg, just a little, love. There. Does that feel all right?"

"Yes." She panted, unsure what he was doing, but she wanted that shattering feeling so badly, she was willing to do whatever he wanted. Her back was to him, her leg draped over his hip. Then something—not his hand—prodded at her opening. Yesterday this would have frightened her unimaginably. Now, however, with his hand still rubbing that incredible little spot, she felt too good to be frightened.

Sandy adjusted himself, then there was pressure and fullness as he entered her, flowing strongly forward until he lay completely inside her.

Her panting grew more frenzied, and she grasped his hand, needing to reassure him and herself. "I'm fine. Truly I am...just don't stop."

Grunting, Sandy withdrew, and she thought he hadn't understood, until he rocked back into her, slowly building a rhythm that started the coiling sensation all over again.

She'd begun to understand that ebb and flow, to rock against him as he thrust in, meeting him each time, slowly intensifying the throbbing within her. Groaning, she tried to speed up, unaccountably wanting to shatter while he was inside her.

"Isabelle?"

"Don't stop. Oh, please, don't stop." Gasping, she strained

against him.

Suddenly, he surged forward, cried out her name and her throbbing core shattered at last. Isabelle spun into a rapturous state, even greater than the time before, because her body could now grasp Sandy's over and over.

Then, as before, she registered a wonderful contentment before the inevitable darkness descended once more.

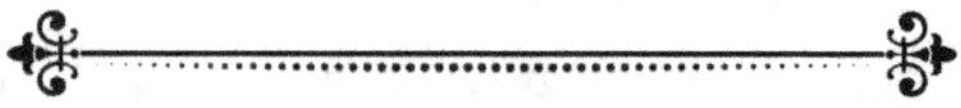

CHAPTER FIFTEEN

Carnwath, Scotland
Six weeks later
Mid-November

"IT HAPPENED AGAIN, didn't it?" Isabelle smiled and snuggled her back up next to Sandy. "I was certain it wouldn't after last night."

Sweaty and spent, Sandy wrapped his arms around his equally sweaty wife, kissing her neck and tasting salt. "I feared I might faint this time as well, my love." His exertions in their latest love play had resulted in a prolonged release that had drained him. Never before in the six weeks since they wed had he come this close to *la petite mort* himself.

"Don't you think that's logical?" Isabelle turned toward him and settled against him again. "When I didn't swoon after last night's deed of pleasure, I could have sworn I wouldn't do it again." She ran her fingers lightly down his chest, dipping one into his navel, making him shudder.

"I didn't think it bothered you anymore, sweetheart." He arrested her hand before it could stray lower and cause any more mischief.

"It doesn't, really, but I do enjoy being able to share those moments just after we…do the deed and not wake up five minutes later to discover you are asleep, my love." Isabelle pouted, her lips in a perfect position for kissing.

They made his dead member stir miraculously. "Well, I'm not asleep now, am I?" He rolled over, pinning her beneath him. "Shall we see if you can remain awake this time?"

Isabelle squealed, then pulled his head down for a kiss.

A sharp rap at the door froze them both. Groaning, Sandy hung his head. Of all the luck. "Bring the tea back in half an hour, Grant."

"It's a telegram just arrived, my lord. From London." The butler's muffled voice sounded concerned.

Isabelle went rigid beneath him and Sandy immediately rolled off her. He hopped to the floor. "A moment, please."

Sandy padded to the chair, grabbed his robe and hastily tugged it on. "Do not concern yourself, my love." He pulled his belt around the dressing gown. "It is likely nothing more than notification that one of my cousins is getting married. I'm assuming their hunts for wives are going on apace."

The sight of Isabelle's ashen face sent a thrill of anger through his body. Her stepfather's presence was never far away it seemed. Sandy went to the door, ruminating that Captain Ambrose Grey needed to stay the hell out of Sandy's bedroom. He paused, ran a hand through his hair, trying to make himself respectable, and opened the door.

Grant handed him the telegram. "Shall I bring the tea tray now, my lord?"

Sandy glanced back at his wife, covers pulled up over her head. "Yes, please. You might as well send breakfast up too, Grant. Has my mother risen yet? She must be exhausted from her journey yesterday."

"Yes, my lord. Her ladyship breakfasted an hour ago and is now writing letters in the morning room. Shall I give her a message?"

Shaking his head, Sandy turned to Isabelle. "My mother is a complete marvel. Indefatigable." Then to Grant. "No, there's nothing at the moment. Tell Hobbes I won't require him for another hour. Neither will Cooper be required until then." If this telegram proved to be word about Captain Grey, he'd need time to reassure his wife.

"Very good, my lord." Grant bowed and Sandy shut the door, gazing at the letter's yellow envelope with trepidation. Grey had attempted to contact Isabelle several times since they had moved to Scotland. The first attempt, a letter in an innocent plain white envelope, had upset his wife so much Sandy had hesitated to give her the second one when it arrived two weeks later. Neither missive had said more than he missed his stepdaughter and wished to know when she'd next be in London.

Sandy dreaded the day a letter or telegram would arrive announcing the man himself was arriving in Carnwath to visit his stepdaughter. He doubted Isabelle would be able to gainsay him, especially if he brought her mother with him. Isabelle would be hard put to refuse such a visit, but Grey's presence would absolutely terrify Sandy's wife. He tapped the envelope against his other hand as he headed back to bed.

"What does it say?" The voice under the cover sounded apprehensive.

"Just a moment, love." Gritting his teeth, Sandy pulled the single sheet out of the envelope and read it—then laughed out loud.

"What does it say?" Isabelle flung the covers off and sat up so suddenly her breasts bounced.

Distracted by that movement, Sandy licked his lips and jumped back into bed. "My cousin, Alex Bancroft, has made a wager—"

"Oh, for goodness sakes!" His wife flopped back onto the mattress. "How dare he frighten me so with a telegram about a silly wager?"

"Silly or not, my lady—" Sandy pounced on her, causing her to shriek, then laugh. "—the wager will call us to London in two weeks' time."

"Why do we need to go to London?" Isabelle sobered. "If I go, I'll have to see Ambrose and my mother. They will know I'm in Town."

"You don't have to see your mother or stepfather ever again if you don't want to, my love."

Gazing up at him, she worried her bottom lip. "I don't know, Sandy. He will find a way to see me."

"Then simply don't go, sweetheart." He kissed the tip of her nose. "Stay here in Scotland with Mother. I need to go to support Alexander—he's fighting in a boxing match and the wagering will be sharp, I guarantee it. Quartermains always support one another."

"Especially when wagering is a part of it, I suspect." Isabelle glared at him.

"I will sorely miss your company, love, but I will understand if you can't go." After six weeks of wedded bliss and constant marital congress, he'd do more than just miss Isabelle. He'd pine every day for her, but he wouldn't subject her to the strain of a possible meeting with that monster unless she wished it.

Isabelle clutched him to her fiercely, as though he might try to leave this minute. "No, Sandy. Where you go, I go. I don't ever wish for us to be apart, my love. I'd miss you too terribly."

"And I you." He kissed her lips, ultimately glad that they would not have to be parted. "What about this? We will travel to London, but we won't tell anyone save my cousin Julius. He requires an answer, but otherwise no one need know we will be in Town. I'm sorry you won't be able to see your mother, but if you don't wish a confrontation with Grey, it's the only way."

The captain was proving to be more of a thorn in Sandy's side than he'd realized. While in London, he'd talk to his family and see what might be done to alleviate it. His grandfather had so many connections perhaps he would have an idea of how to deal with the man.

Smiling, Sandy lowered his lips to his wife's mouth. After a prolonged kiss that made him harden immediately, he grinned at her. "Are you up for a wager of our own?"

"Perhaps." Cheeks flushed, she ground her hips into him. "What is it?"

Sandy groaned. "I wager I can make you faint again before breakfast arrives."

December 1

"Let us go in here, Lady MacKay, away from all the din." Emma Bancroft led Isabelle into a small receiving room, cozily furnished with a roaring fire against the damp December chill. "You don't know how good it is to have another woman to talk to at these Quartermain gatherings. So far it's only been me and Emily, Harry's wife, but she's so far along in the family way, we won't see her until the spring."

"I wondered why I hadn't met her yet." Isabelle chose the chair nearest the fire. Emma sat across from her on a small chaise. "My husband told me his cousin's marriage to Emily sparked a wager that we are now both part of."

"Yes, thank goodness. Eventually there will be seven of us cousins-in-law." Emma laughed gaily. "We will have more fun together than our husbands will, I daresay." Her cousin-in-law's high spirits had caught Isabelle's attention at the party in the ballroom. That room had unfortunate memories for her, so she'd wanted to sneak away and found Emma a willing conspirator.

"I am certain you are much relieved now that your husband has won his wager." Isabelle had been horrified to discover Emma had donned men's clothing and actually attended the brutal boxing match where her husband and his uncle had fought. Rather than be sent to India and separated from Emma for five years, her husband Alex had instead resigned his commission in the Army and taken a wager on a boxing match at his uncle's urging. If Alex won, he'd be given an estate and money to live on.

If he lost, he and Emma would travel to the north where Alex would have to teach boxing in a new unit dedicated to physical fitness.

"How could you do it, Mrs. Bancroft? How did you dare dress so scandalously and attend the match when your husband had forbidden it?"

"Please do call me Emma." Her cousin-in-law leaned over and patted her hand. "We are family, after all."

"Of course, Emma. And you must call me Isabelle. But how could you be so daring?"

"With mine and Alex's future and happiness in the balance, I couldn't stand by and simply wait for him to return and inform me of the outcome." Emma shrugged. "I needed to act because it was my future being decided. I also needed to know Alex was safe. I couldn't just sit home and wait like a ninny wringing my hands."

Isabelle gave her an arch look. "What did your husband say when he found out?"

Emma's cheeks grew rosy. "He wasn't very happy with me at all. And I suspect I'll continue to feel the sting of his tongue whenever we're in private for some time to come. All in all, however, I think gentlemen like a woman with spunk, no matter how much they may protest they don't."

"There you are, my dear." Alex Bancroft, tall, handsome, and sporting a black eye from his boxing match, sauntered into the room. "Good evening, cousin." He bowed to Isabelle. "May I steal my wife for a moment? Grandfather wants to have a word with her regarding her recent foray into the world of boxing."

"Goodness, Emma, that sounds ominous." Isabelle was more than a little frightened of the imposing Duke of Welwyn, even though he'd congratulated her on keeping her promise and helping Sandy with his part of the marriage wager.

"I assure you, my wife can handle him." He glared at Emma playfully. "It's me she needs to worry about."

"Then I don't need to worry at all, do I, my love?" Emma

smiled into his face. "Will you come with us, Isabelle?"

"No, thank you. I am perfectly fine here, but if you see my husband, would you send him to me?"

"Of course. I saw him just now with Julius, settling their accounts." Alex took Emma's hand, his gaze never leaving her face. "Come, my dear. Grandfather is a very important man. We mustn't keep him waiting." He led her from the room and Isabelle settled back in the comfortable chair to enjoy the warmth of the fire while she awaited her husband.

They had been in Town for two days leading up to this boxing match, Sandy becoming more and more excited as the event drew closer. She smiled thinking of his enthusiasm, so like all the Quartermains she'd become re-acquainted with during that time. Sandy had been right, they were all fools for a wager.

Perhaps tonight she'd have to place a wager of her own with her husband. A very private wager regarding how long it would take her to—

"Isabelle."

That voice froze her blood in her veins. She jerked her head up and met the black eyes of Ambrose Grey. Her heart gave a great leap as though trying to escape on its own, then beat with the frantic rhythm of a bird battering its wings against the bars of a cage. "Wha…what are you doing here?"

"I've come to see you, of course, my dear." To her horror he entered the parlor and shut the door.

She jumped to her feet, but there was nowhere to go.

"We hardly spoke after I returned in September, then you were off to the North, then married." He eased into the chaise Emma had sat on and smiled, showing his yellowing teeth. The years on the island had taken a toll on his appearance. "Sit down, Isabelle."

The harsh tone of the command brought back all the terror of the years of his abuse. And conditioned to obey, she duly sat down, feeling like a mouse in the company of a hungry cat.

"When I heard about the match with your Quartermain

relations, I assumed your husband would attend." The grotesque smile widened. "And bring you with him."

Despite her roiling stomach, Isabelle tried to remain calm. "Now you have seen me, Ambrose, and as I have nothing to say to you other than goodbye—Ouch!" She rose, meaning to head to the door, but he grabbed her arm so roughly, she winced.

"Not so fast, my dear. We have some plans to make, you and I."

Isabelle twisted her arm, trying to break his hold, but the man's strength was too much for her. Well, there were other ways than force. "I have only to scream and all the Quartermains—including my husband—will be in here in moments."

"Oh, but you surely don't want to do that, Isabelle. You surely don't." He fixed her with his evil, dark-eyed gaze, and all the strength drained out of her legs. Whatever imp from hell inhabited her stepfather's soul, it was making itself known right now, ready to set some diabolical plot into play. "I'm certain you'd have a care not to endanger your mother's precarious health."

"My mother?" Isabelle collapsed into the chair and he let her arm go. She rubbed the place where bruises were already forming. "What is wrong with Mama?"

"She knew you were here in London and neglected to tell me." He shook his head. "She knows better than to keep secrets from her husband. I had to correct that behavior last night until at last she admitted she had known of your presence."

"But she didn't!" The protest came quickly, much good it would do her mother. God only knew what he'd done to her already. "We told no one I was coming. Not even the Quartermains knew."

"Truly? Tsk, tsk. I must apologize to your mother for doubting her word."

Isabelle shuddered. Ambrose never apologized to anyone. "You are a fiend, Ambrose Grey. You leave my mother alone."

"Watch your tongue, girl." He leaned toward her, menace in

his tone. "Who are you to tell me what to do?"

"I am Lady MacKay, Captain Grey." She sprang to her feet, but careful to move out of his reach. "I now have the power of my husband's position and family ties behind me. If you touch me, they will bring the full weight of the law to bear on you." She wasn't certain that was true, but it seemed like a threat Ambrose might respect.

"Now listen closely, *Lady MacKay*." His sneer made her want to cower, but somehow, she stood her ground. "Your husband's family may be able to protect you, but they can't do a thing about how I treat my wife. The law says a man can chastise his wife for misbehavior. Which means I can beat her, as long as I don't break her bones or cause irreparable harm." He grinned at her and Isabelle thought she'd swoon at the evil looking out of his eyes. "There are many ways a man can cause a woman pain without 'irreparable harm.' I can even strip her naked and turn her out of the house and the law won't lift a finger against me."

Tears pricked Isabelle's eyes at the image of her mother broken and degraded at the hands of the monster she had married. "Then what do you want, Ambrose? Do you want to come have tea with me here in Welwyn House? Whatever you want, I will do if you will leave my mother alone."

"My dear, I want what I have always wanted." He gazed at her with lust laden eyes. "I want you to be my mistress."

As though she was falling from a great height, Isabelle's head spun as a great roaring filled her ears. Everything in the room wavered until—

Crack!

Her cheek exploded with pain. She jerked upright, coming face to face with Ambrose.

"We don't have time for swooning, my dear. You need to listen to me and listen good. I mean to meet you here tomorrow afternoon to take you out in the carriage. Tell your husband you have reconciled with me for your mother's sake and I am taking you to her so we can all three clear the air between us."

Isabelle touched her cheek gingerly, hoping the fire would die down soon. It usually did, if the attack wasn't repeated. She'd endured such things before.

The smile on his face turned into a lustful leer. "Of course, we will instead go to a house I've rented, just for the two of us."

Bile rose up in her throat, but she choked it back. "You must be mad to think I would do such a thing." He could strike her mother true, but when Sandy saw the bruises on her arm and face, Ambrose would be lucky to survive his wrath. "You have both assaulted and made vile suggestions to the wife of a peer. Such offenses are not above the law."

"They may not be, but if you tell your husband or any of his kinfolk about this, or about our little arrangement, I promise you I'll make your mother's life a living hell. There are things I will do to her, Isabelle. Things you cannot even imagine. Things that will make her beg for death."

Her breath came in shallow gasps now, unable to take in enough air. Soon she would swoon in earnest, a small respite from the nightmare that had come to life before her.

Ambrose's evil smile emerged again. "I trust a daughter who loved her mother wouldn't stand by and let that happen when she could so easily prevent it."

Fear closed Isabelle's throat so tightly, she thought she was choking. She couldn't let this fiend torture her mother. Neither could she allow herself to be sullied and defiled by him as she betrayed her most loving husband. Gazing into Grey's eyes which were devoid of any feeling save lust, she had no doubt at all he would carry out his threat until she gave in and became his mistress.

"Shall I call around here about one o'clock tomorrow?" His tone was the same as if he were asking her to a picnic in the park. "Then we can have a nice, *long* afternoon, just the two of us. You'll even be home in time for tea."

The hopelessness of the situation hit Isabelle with the power of a cannonball exploding in the midst of her idyllic life. Once she began this affair, she suspected he would never let her go. "Lord MacKay plans to leave London in a few days. How do I know my mother will be safe once I have returned to Scotland?"

"An intelligent wife would persuade her husband that her mother's precarious health necessitates your regular visits to her bedside. Say, one week out of each month." He leaned back in his chair, obviously pleased with himself. "I'm certain a young bride can prevail upon her doting husband to allow such journeys for some time to come."

Oh, no. He'd not let her go. Ever. Then this was the choice she must make. Her mother's life or her husband's honor.

It really was no choice at all when she thought of it like that. Summoning all her courage, Isabelle nodded. "You can pick me up here, at one o'clock tomorrow. The butler will show you to this room. It's where all callers are received. We can leave from here. As long as I am back in time for tea, nothing will be thought amiss."

Ambrose's grin widened. "I knew you would see the sense of this, my dear. You are satisfied to keep your mother safe, and I will be satisfied…in so many ways." Eyes unfocused, he stared at her, seeming not to see her, but something else. "When I was marooned on that godforsaken island for so long, I thought about you every day, every night. Thought about what I would do when I was finally in bed with you again." He licked his lips and focused his gaze on her. "Tomorrow, I'll show you what I thought about doing to you most often."

Finally numb to his disgusting intimations, Isabelle rose. "I must go or I'll be missed. I will be here tomorrow without fail."

"As will I, my dear." Ambrose grasped her hand, pulling it to his lips.

Isabelle snatched it away, ran to the door, pulled it open, then fled down the corridor. Sick to her stomach and sick at heart, she raced for her bedchamber, not knowing what she was going to do, yet knowing she had to find some way out of this never-ending nightmare.

CHAPTER SIXTEEN

AFTER MAKING SURE Ambrose had left the premises, Isabelle pled a headache and went directly to their chamber. Cooper helped her into her nightgown and brushed her hair until the soothing motion calmed Isabelle enough to be able to think clearly.

What was she going to do?

"Shall I bring you some supper, my lady?" The maid had tidied the chamber and stood ready for her next chore.

"No, thank you. I am not hungry." Her stomach might well revolt at any moment. "You may go for the night."

"Are you certain, my lady? You don't look at all well." Her maid knew her well enough by now to know when something was amiss.

"I'm tired, that's all." Weary beyond belief, Isabelle moved to the bed. She needed time to think before Sandy retired for the night. He would likely play cards with his cousins until late, which would give Isabelle that very necessary—

"Did I hear you plan not to dine with us, my dear?" The door had opened revealing Sandy, a frown marring his handsome face. "Are you not well?"

"Thank you, Cooper. You may go."

With a searching look at her mistress, the maid left, shutting the door.

Summoning a smile, Isabelle patted the covers beside her. "Come sit here, my love."

He bounded over to the bed and sat carefully next to her. "Are you simply tired from all the excitement and traveling? Or is something the matter?"

"Do not worry, Sandy. I believe it is the traveling mostly. And of course, being in the midst of Quartermains and their wagers would be a drain on anyone. I take it you made some canny wagers?"

Her husband beamed at her, totally distracted from her welfare, as she had hoped. "I did. In fact, I won against Grandfather, which is no mean feat."

"Then perhaps we should celebrate your victory." Isabelle hadn't planned on this encounter, however it would be the last time she could make love to her husband without the crushing guilt of the betrayal she was about to perpetrate on him. It would also be the last chance for them to conceive a child for the foreseeable future.

After Ambrose was presumed dead, her mother had spoken to her of a tea she'd drunk each morning that would keep a woman barren. Mama hadn't wanted to bring a child into a world of fear and violence. Now Isabelle would need to do the same. That she might one day bear a child that wasn't Sandy's was as abhorrent as the act she was about to commit. But if she was to save her mother's life, what else could she do?

"Are you sure, sweetheart?" Sandy's worried face searched hers intently. "I was told you had a headache."

"Because I knew that excuse would allow me to come here." Isabelle raised her brows in what she hoped was a seductive manner. "And wait for you. If you had tarried too long downstairs, I would have sent Cooper to find you." She slid her arms around his neck and pulled his mouth to hers. "As I said, a celebration is in order."

Grinning broadly, Sandy quickly gathered her in his arms, deepening the kiss immediately. He explored her mouth thoroughly, tasting her even as she savored the slight sweetness of a peppermint he'd apparently eaten. They were his favorite. Lost in the kiss, Isabelle allowed herself simply to enjoy the pleasure he gave her.

Too soon he broke the kiss, but only to strip off his clothing, tossing it piece by piece around the room. She giggled when his cravat caught on the pitcher standing on the washstand. Cooper had forgotten to put the screen back around it. The cravat draped jauntily over the handle, a whimsical come-hither air to it.

When she turned her attention back to her husband, he'd stripped to his shirt, which then came tearing off over his head, revealing his beautiful body—broad chest, narrow waist tapering to slim hips. And of course, his cock jutting out magnificently. She could gaze at him for hours had she been given the chance.

However, sight of his arousal always made her nether regions heat and throb. Tonight, she wanted him so badly, she stroked its length boldly, making him shiver.

"You are a minx, wife. You know exactly how to make me ready for you in an instant." He swept the covers off her then pushed her nightgown up over her stomach. "I, however, have something else in mind first."

Isabelle strained upward, seeking his mouth again, but it was gone—suddenly descending to her navel. She gasped as he ran his tongue around it, dipping into the shallow hole, nibbling at her flesh, making her gasp and moan.

"You like that, do you, madam?" He smiled against her skin and continued downward.

Squirming as he inched closer to her nether regions, Isabelle held her breath, disbelieving what he seemed to be aiming to… "What…what are you doing?"

"Something I think you will like very much, my love." He'd raised his head to speak, then lowered his mouth to her most private place.

"Sandy!"

"Hmm?" His togue slid all around, making her pant furiously.

"Sandy...what...oh, goodness...ahhh!" Her body was on fire, aching for his tongue to continue with whatever it wanted to do.

"Do you wish me to stop?"

"No...ohhh nooo...nooo..." Everything he was doing gave her more and more pleasure. Made her feel like she would explode in that delicious way any second now.

Then he touched his tongue to the little pearl he sometimes stroked with his finger, which almost always brought on her release. This time he licked the little button, swirled his tongue around it and she moaned deeply in absolute ecstasy. When he sucked the little nub into his mouth and tickled it, Isabelle's world shattered as never before. She was hit with a deep release she felt down to her toes, wave after wave of pleasure breaking over her, ones she never wanted to cease. Each time he sucked, another wave crashed until she lay melted into the sheets, gasping for air. But she hadn't fainted, thank God. She experienced each and every little nuance of it until she lay back limp and sated.

"Did you enjoy that, my love?" She could hear the smile in Sandy's voice and she nodded once, too weak to do more. "Then let's see if we can make this time even better."

"This...time?" Struggling to draw out the words, Isabelle was so drained of her essence she didn't believe him. "So soon?" Speaking had never been such an effort. How could she manage another release?

"Women can achieve release multiple times with little pause. You are much more fortunate than we men in that regard." Quickly, he covered her, his weight pressing her into the mattress in a wonderful, possessive way. His lips fastened onto her nipple, tugged gently, which was more than enough to send streaks of fire down to her still throbbing core.

"You always make me feel so loved, Sandy," she whispered as he slipped inside her, flowing forward until he was seated deeply within. "Oh, Sandy." Her whole body was winding upward to another spectacular release, one that might send her into a permanent swoon.

Plunging into her over and over, deeper and deeper, Sandy alternated sucking on each of her nipples until Isabelle feared she'd go mad with the ecstasy of it. The rhythm built like music toward a shattering crescendo. Her heart pounded in her chest, a counterpoint to his pounding down below. Then he sped up, straining against her, pulling on her nipple until she couldn't help but shatter around him. He called her name frantically as he spent himself on and on, filling her full of his precious essence.

Finally, leaning back on his arms, both of them drenched in sweat, Isabelle could only think that if a child should come of this joining, she was bound to protect it from anything that threatened it or her. No matter what consequences might come from that action. Ambrose Grey would never harm her again.

With that thought foremost in her mind, Isabelle relaxed, and Sandy's protective arms embraced her. She would take Emma's advice to heart, defend her and her husband's future life and happiness. So help her God, no matter what it took, she would keep them all safe from any harm.

MORE CHEERFUL THAN he'd ever believed possible, Sandy had just finished lunch with his grandfather and was now in search of Isabelle who he'd asked to accompany him on a carriage ride to the Kensington Arcade for an afternoon of fun and Christmas shopping. The holiday was weeks away, but they would be leaving for Scotland on Tuesday, so he wanted her to have the advantage of perusing the larger shops when securing presents for his mother and hers.

Sandy pursed his lips. He supposed it would look odd if Isabelle didn't give her stepfather a gift as well, although thoughts of rewarding the man's gross misbehavior stuck in Sandy's craw. Of course, they would be spending Christmas in Scotland, far away from Grey, so any present would be a mere token. He should be able to swallow that much. If only there was some way of getting rid of the man once and for all. Perhaps he should consult with Grandfather. The man was as crafty as they came, not to mention powerful. He might come up with a more permanent solution to the problem of Ambrose Grey.

Heading for the foyer to order the carriage brought around, the sound of muffled voices in the small parlor gave Sandy pause. His grandparents weren't receiving today. Yesterday's entertainment had been more than enough for them.

He motioned the footman attending the door over to him. "Who is in the small parlor, as they are calling it now, George?"

"A Captain Grey called about five minutes ago for Lady MacKay, my lord. He said he was taking her driving."

Sandy froze as though changed into an ice sculpture, staring at the footman as though he'd started speaking Japanese. "Captain Grey has called to take *my* wife driving? Did you send word to Lady MacKay?" The man must be mad to think Isabelle would go anywhere with him. "Has my lady come down yet?"

Something in Sandy's face must have frightened George, for he backed up a step. "Yes, my lord. She went in a minute or two ago."

Before George could finish his sentence, Sandy had grasped the door latch and pushed it down. The door swung open on a tableau so bizarre Sandy had to blink several times to take it in.

Captain Grey stood in front of the fireplace, hands outstretched, his gaze fixed unwaveringly on Isabelle, perhaps two paces from him, a dueling pistol grasped in her shaking hand, the weapon cocked and ready to fire.

Sandy took a long breath, his mind working furiously to decipher the scene before him. He had no idea how proficient his wife was with a gun, but he'd take no chances and so would assume she had no training whatsoever and had never fired one. In that case, he had to try to get her to surrender the gun before it went off and injured her or himself. Grey he was less worried about. The situation reeked of his doing. Now he needed to discern whether Isabelle was merely attempting to frighten her stepfather or actually kill him. He suspected the latter, given the determination etched on her face. "Isabelle, I'm going to walk toward you, my dear." He kept his voice nice and soothing. "Don't move, please."

She gave him a tense nod, though she did not take her gaze off Grey, whose face had gone ashen.

"MacKay, thank God." Grey tried to take a step toward him.

"Stay where you are!" Isabelle screeched, aiming the pistol higher, toward her stepfather's chest. "Don't move."

Step by step, Sandy approached her, unsure if she'd simply snapped at finding Grey in the house. But then, when and how had she gotten the pistol? "I'm right here, Isabelle." He stepped beside her. "Will you allow me to take the weapon, sweetheart?"

Continuing to stare at Grey, his wife shook her head. "He's threatened us, Sandy. He's threatened to do unthinkable things to my mother if I don't become his mistress."

All the blood seemed to rush out of Sandy's body at that horrible pronouncement.

Isabelle clutched the pistol, still aimed at Grey's broad chest, tears trickling down her cheeks. "He needs to die, Sandy. That's the only way we can be safe. The only way we can be free."

"MacKay..." Grey licked his lips, fear in his voice. "You can tell she's deranged by the nonsense she's spewing." He turned pleading eyes on Sandy. "Can you please get that damned pistol away from her before it goes off?"

Cutting his gaze from Grey to Isabelle, Sandy held out his hand. "Please give me the gun, my love. I will take it over until I hear the whole story."

"No!" Isabelle shook her head, not even glancing at him, her focus locked on Grey the entire time. "I have to do this, Sandy. He won't ever stop, don't you see?" Her hand steadied and she became eerily calm. "Unless I stop him."

"Isabelle, no!" Sandy jumped forward just as she smiled and pulled the trigger.

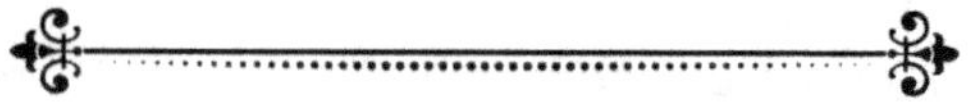

CHAPTER SEVENTEEN

"SO, CAPTAIN GREY arrived uninvited, you say?" Harold Gossing, the London coroner who'd been hastily summoned to Welwyn House, had convened his inquest at The Guinea Tavern not half an hour after Captain Grey had been pronounced dead. The twelve men hired as jurors who would determine if the matter would go to trial sat before the coroner and the witnesses moving restlessly.

"That's what I surmise, Mr. Gossing." Trying to act calm and concerned, Sandy had taken the stand as the first witness. He, along with Isabelle, his grandfather, and George the footman, had been summoned to testify at the inquest. "He was my wife's stepfather. The two had been estranged ever since our marriage, so I doubt anyone in the house would have invited him in." Sandy was determined to keep as much of the truth in his story as possible, but it was devilishly difficult as he still wasn't certain exactly what had transpired between Isabelle and Grey. He'd been unable to get much out of Isabelle before the shot she fired brought servants and family members running.

"When you came into the room, she and Captain Grey were arguing?" The coroner looked up from his hastily scratched notes.

"No, not arguing. My wife was crying hysterically, terribly upset, as she told me later, at some things the captain had threatened to do to her mother—his wife—if Lady MacKay refused to reconcile with him." That was as close to the truth as Sandy intended to get. He stared pointedly at his wife, willing her to remain silent.

Face pale, Isabelle shifted uncomfortably on the tavern bench. Her eyes, red from weeping, looked sore, but she lifted her chin and nodded infinitesimally.

Sandy then shifted his gaze to his grandfather, who sat stoically to the side with the footman. In the carriage on the way to the inquest, Grandfather had intimated he wished to put the full authority of his title and station on display for the coroner. With his sober countenance and piercing gaze, he couldn't have been more imposing if he'd been wearing his ducal robes and coronet. Grandfather nodded at Sandy, who sighed in relief. Grandfather was the only other person to whom Sandy had confided the truth about the encounter this morning, including Grey's perverted demand to Isabelle. His grandfather's only comment had been that he wished he'd have been the one to pull the trigger.

"So Captain Grey was attempting to extort Lady MacKay with the promise of violence against her mother if she did not cooperate in the reconciliation?" Gossing's face remained neutral, although his gaze flicked over Sandy's face.

"That is correct." Sandy struggled to maintain a bland countenance, despite the raging anger that bubbled up each time he thought of Grey's monstrous demand. "He had been violent with my wife before he left home in 1857. She feared a return to the same behavior if she acquiesced to a reconciliation." Sandy hesitated over offering the next piece of evidence but believed it would help in the end. "You can see bruises on my wife's arm where he grabbed her." He would have words for Isabelle when this was over regarding the marks on her arm, marks she'd claimed the night before had been made by a footman who had caught her when she slipped on the staircase. "I don't know what would have happened to her had I not come into the room when I did."

"And when you came upon them, you happened to be carrying a pistol?" The coroner shot him a keen look. "Are you in the habit of carrying loaded firearms about the house?"

Grandfather leaned forward as if he meant to rebuke the man for his flippant remark.

Sandy gave a subtle shake of his head, and Grandfather sat back, none too pleased. "No, Mr. Gossing, of course I'm not. My family, however, *is* in the habit of wagering on a wide variety of things. My cousins and I had been discussing a recent wager at one of our clubs where the ability to hit a mark in the exact same place three times in a row had been in question. So of course, we wished to try our hand at such a wager. I'd been sent to the library for the pistol and was heading out to the front lawn where we were going to set up the marks, when I heard voices and asked a footman about it. He told me my wife was in there and when I opened the door, I came upon the scene I previously described."

"You saw him assaulting Lady MacKay?"

"No, but he apparently had done so, perhaps trying to force her to leave with him." Sandy threw up his hands. "What was I supposed to do? My wife was crying hysterically, Grey was close to her, shouting at her. I warned him away, but he didn't seem to hear or care. I pointed the weapon at him, but he refused to back away. He took a step toward her so… I rushed toward them and the gun went off."

Gossing glanced at him with narrowed eyes. "You didn't think to call for assistance?"

"Lady MacKay was in tears. The brute was bearing down on her." Sandy shrugged. "There was no time to do anything but act, Mr. Gossing. So I acted as any husband would to protect his wife and in the confusion, the gun fired."

Gossing stared at him steadily, then finally said, "The witness may step down." He shuffled some papers, then looked up. "I call Lady MacKay to the witness box, please."

Looking as though she'd burst into tears at any moment, Isabelle rose just as Sandy sat down on the bench beside her.

"Don't worry my love. Just tell them what happened." He prayed his meaningful glance wasn't lost on his wife.

The minute he'd taken the pistol from her hand that morning, he'd insisted he would take responsibility.

"You will allow me to do this, Isabelle. If you are called, tell the absolute truth about everything else, but you will say that I was the one who fired the shot."

"But why, Sandy?" Her face had been puffy from so many tears. "I was the one who shot him."

"Because no matter how much we may believe you were justified to do so, my love, you could be tried for murder." He shook his head, his heart tearing apart at the thought. "You took the pistol there in order to shoot him."

"To threaten him. I…I didn't know I was going to shoot him." She'd sobbed anew. "But I suddenly didn't see any other way to make him leave us alone." She'd looked so hopelessly confused, all he could do was hold her close, even as servants and his cousins raced into the room. "Why won't they arrest you if I say you killed him?" She dissolved into tears again. "Sandy, I don't understand."

"Trust me, my love. Just trust me."

God, he hoped she trusted him enough to let him take the blame for this debacle.

Slowly, Isabelle walked to the witness stand, her gaze fixed on Mr. Gossing.

"Now, Lady MacKay, I know you've had quite a shock this morning. But can you tell me what exactly happened?" To give him credit, Mr. Gossing had softened his voice considerably.

"One of the footmen told me there was a caller in the front receiving room, but the gentleman refused to leave his name. When I arrived, I discovered it was my stepfather, Captain Grey."

"What did he say to you, my lady?"

Isabelle closed her eyes. "He said he wanted me to reconcile with him and my mother, and if I refused, he would make my mother wish she was dead."

"And you took this to mean...?" Gossing peered closely at her.

Isabelle's eyes snapped open. "He meant he would beat her until she was black and blue—as he's done so many times before. You have no idea what we suffered under his roof, Mr. Gossing." She stared at the jurors, most of whom refused to look at her. "He wasn't going to stop until he got his way."

"Lord MacKay says that Captain Grey grabbed your arm and bruised it. May I see it, please?" Mr. Gossing stood, peering at Isabelle while she pulled up the undersleeve of her gown revealing the ugly, discolored flesh in the shape of a full handprint wrapped around her left arm.

Sandy fought the urge to sink his fist into something. Grey was dead and it would do his case no good for him to punch a wall. Still, he ached to avenge his wife's hurts in a more concrete way.

"Thank you, Lady MacKay." The coroner sat back down, making more notes on the papers before him. "What happened when your husband entered the room?"

"I'm not actually certain at what point he did enter it. The whole thing is such a blur." Isabelle put her hand to her forehead. "I only know I was crying, and Captain Grey was shouting at me to go with him, and I began to think there was no way to make it all stop." She looked back at Sandy, her eyes tearing up again. "And then my husband was there and I was so relieved. I knew he would help me. He always has."

"And then what happened?"

Staring at Mr. Gossing, Isabelle shrugged. "There was a shot. I really didn't know where it came from. Then Captain Grey was on the floor and my husband had me safe in his arms." Tears poured down her face and she sobbed into her handkerchief. "I am so sorry my love, for what he put us through."

"Now, now, Lady MacKay." Mr. Gossing looked ill-at-ease. He motioned to Sandy. "Will you escort your wife from the box, my lord. I believe we have heard as much as we need." He shot a keen look at the jurors.

Putting his arm around his wife's shoulders, Sandy paused to peer at the jurors who had huddled together in the jury box. Had they gained sympathy for them from Isabelle's testimony?

"Just a moment, if you please."

Sandy jerked his head up as his grandfather strode forward, a determined look in his eyes.

"I have evidence I believe the courts should consider regarding this matter, Mr. Gossing." Grandfather handed a letter to the coroner. "You did not call me to testify, else I would have given this to you then."

Frowning, Sandy peered at his grandfather and mouthed the words, "What is it?"

Grandfather merely smiled and turned back to the coroner, who was avidly perusing the letter. He looked up at the duke, a stunned looked on his face. "How did you come by this letter, Your Grace?"

"When Captain Grey returned so miraculously, I wished to verify his account of his rescue. With my grandson marrying his stepdaughter, I needed to make certain of his *bona fides*, you understand." The pious look on Grandfather's face would have fooled no one in the family, but apparently went a long way to convincing Mr. Gossing. "I sent out inquiries to the owner of the *Cordelia*, and was amazed when this letter appeared not a week ago." He turned to look at Sandy, one eyebrow quirked up. "Will you read it for the jury, please, Mr. Gossing?"

The coroner spread the letter out on the table. "My Lord Duke, I write at your express command with information about Captain Ambrose Grey and the incident that occurred on my company's ship, the *Cordelia*. One month into the ship's return passage from Jamaica three years ago, Captain Grey became enraged when his cabin boy stumbled, spilling hot soup on the captain in his cabin. Grey reportedly grabbed the boy by the scruff of the neck, hauled him out of the cabin and up on deck and before anyone could stop him, heaved the unfortunate lad over the railing and into the sea."

There was a collective gasp from everyone present and Isabelle buried her face in Sandy's chest. Had he known of this atrocity before now, Sandy wouldn't have waited to confront Grey with a pistol in hand.

With a gulp, Mr. Gossing continued. "Stunned, the rest of the crew made every effort to rescue the child, but he disappeared under the waves before they could save him. At this point, it is apparent from the logbook that the crew mutinied." The coroner looked up at the jury, all of whom were raptly listening, if somewhat pale. "They bound Captain Grey hand and foot, then the next morning rowed him out to an uninhabited island in the Canaries and put him ashore, thinking this would dissipate any ill luck the captain's gruesome actions might have brought upon them. But the *Cordelia* was apparently ill-fated to the end."

With such a hand at the mast as Grey, Sandy wasn't surprised the ship was cursed.

"A wild storm came up not long after they abandoned their captain and the ship broke apart off the coast of Funchal. All hands were lost, and I had no idea what had happened to the ship until about a year ago when pieces of flotsam and jetsam washed up on shore, one piece of which was stamped with my company's name. I was contacted and sent a ship to try to salvage as much as possible. Along with some barrels of goods, they recovered the logbook, sealed in oilcloth, so we at least know what occurred aboard the *Cordelia*. I trust you will make these matters known to the authorities at the proper time and Captain Grey will be brought to justice for his inhuman crime. I remain Your Grace's most obedient servant, Phillip S. Samuels." Mr. Gossing straightened in his chair and turned to the jury. "Based on the evidence presented, has the jury reached a verdict?"

The men looked at one another and nodded together. One burly gentleman stood up and faced the coroner. "Mr. Gossing, we find insufficient evidence to rule this a homicide. We find instead the manner of death should be ruled death by misadventure." The man looked steadily at Sandy and Isabelle. "Captain Grey appears to have acted with the intent to forcibly remove Lady MacKay from the premises, God alone knows for what nefarious purpose. During such action, a shot was accidentally discharged causing Grey's demise."

"Thank you, Mr. Potter." Mr. Gossing nodded and the jury began to disperse. "Lord MacKay, Lady MacKay." He offered the letter back to Grandfather. "Your Grace. The cause of death is officially ruled as death by misadventure and the case is closed."

"Thank you, Mr. Gossing." Grandfather tucked the letter back in his pocket, a hint of a smirk on his face.

"Thank you, Mr. Gossing." Sandy hugged Isabelle close to him. A huge weight rolled from his shoulders. As soon as they got home, they needed to light a candle in thanks to God. Without divine intervention, things could have gone so much worse for both of them. "Let's go home, sweetheart."

Isabelle nodded, her head against his chest. "I'm so tired. I feel as though I've been trudging through mud forever."

"All that is behind us now, my love." Sandy kissed her head. "We have only the best of our lives ahead of us."

Grandfather fell into step as they left the inn. "Be assured of that, my dear. If you and my grandson can weather this hurricane, you will live a long and happy life."

Sandy glanced up at the older man, whose spry step was making Sandy work to keep up. "So you had suspicions about Grey even before this, Grandfather?"

"In my experience, my boy, miracles are usually less miraculous than they seem." He shrugged. "It seemed prudent to investigate the man if he was going to be part of my great-grandchild's life."

"Great-grandchild?" Sandy looked askance up at his grandfather. "We've scarcely been married two months."

His grandfather grinned. "You're a Quartermain, Sandy. Blood will tell."

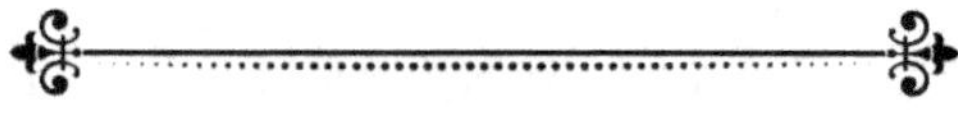

Epilogue

SNOW COVERED THE ground several inches thick on Christmas Day as Isabelle gazed out over the beautiful, crystallized landscape from the second-floor drawing room at Cridhe Laidir. She and Sandy and both their mothers were spending the holiday quietly, although Isabelle couldn't have wished for a more festive celebration. Her mother was, of course, ostensibly in mourning for Ambrose, although she, Sandy and his mother all protested she'd mourned him well enough three years ago and that should suffice. Mama wasn't certain she agreed with that, for some reason. However, as the last batch of massive bruises inflicted upon her by her late husband were healing slowly, she was content to be confined to the castle walls. That way the public wouldn't know about the abuse and she wouldn't have to wear all the outward signs of mourning, such as that awful crepe. Inside the castle, she was wearing half-mourning colors, which Isabelle thought a perfect compromise for a man no one genuinely mourned.

They had gathered at the Christmas tree after Cook's splendid Christmas dinner of roasted goose with all the trimmings, now ready to exchange gifts one by one.

"This one is for you, Mama, from Sandy and me." Isabelle held out a large square wrapped box.

Laughing, Mama took it and shook it quite like a child.

"Whatever can it be?" She swiftly unwrapped the gay paper and opened the box to find a necklace of fiery opals set in gold. "Oh, Isabelle, Sandy, I cannot thank you enough." Mama held them up to her neck, entranced. "But where will I ever wear them?"

"Never fear, Mrs. Grey." Sandy's eyes twinkled. "We intend to take you to London in the spring to show you off."

To show that she'd survived her brute of a husband and therefore deserved to enjoy some time in Town.

"And this is for you, Mother." Sandy handed a similar box to Lady MacKay, which turned out to be an amethyst parure set in gold with jet accents. "You will also accompany us to London. It's about time you enjoyed yourself as well." Sandy kissed his mother's cheek.

In the five years since his father's untimely death, his mother had had to force herself to take any kind of interest in life at Cridhe Laidir. Their love had been so strong Sandy had feared for a time he'd lose her too, from sheer grief. Now that he had Isabelle, he understood how that might happen much better than before. Fortunately, Quatermains were made of tempered steel, stronger and tougher than most. Mother had weathered the worst and now that he was poised to give her the grandchild she'd set her heart on, he hoped she'd begin to take more of an interest in life and particularly in Society again.

"We will see about that, Sandy," was all she'd say, but her face had lit up at the prospect of attending the Season once again.

"You and Sandy haven't exchanged gifts yet, my dear," Mama spoke up when the discarded paper and ribbons had been collected and the coffee had been handed around.

"We exchanged our gifts earlier, Mama." Isabelle blushed but turned to Sandy laughing. They'd enjoyed the pleasures of their bed this Christmas morning until they'd both lay sated in the early light. Had Isabelle gotten no other gift, their continued intimacy would have been the best present she could have received. Of course, they couldn't say that to their mothers.

"Sandy's present from me is out in the barn, a new black

stallion for his stable. And this was Sandy's gift to me." She flashed a huge square-cut diamond ring with rubies on either side. It sparkled outrageously whenever the light hit it.

They sat enjoying their coffee, sharing stories from previous Christmases until there was a lull in the conversation.

"I must warn you, Isabelle and Mrs. Grey, that Christmas here in Scotland is much more sedate than the Hogmanay celebrations coming up." Sandy drained his cup. "Next week you'll see just how rowdy we can be to usher in the New Year. To which end I have already set a wager with Julius that we will be parents by the end of September."

"Oh, Sandy, you didn't." Isabelle blushed to think her husband had spoken of such a thing to his cousin.

"Do not be distraught, my dear," Lady MacKay spoke up, a rueful look in her eyes. "The Quartermains wager on everything. Even things quite delicate in nature. The longer you are part of the family, the more you will discover it is the wager that matters, not decorum or proper sensibilities."

"You were the same way, Mother. Don't deny it." Sandy laughed and patted his mother's hands.

"Did you ever hear me deny it, Saunders?" His mother sipped her coffee, giving him what Sandy had told her he called "the look."

"Perhaps then I should get in on the wager as well," Isabelle smiled agreeably at her husband. "Although I will lay my wager that we will become parents no later than…" She looked at the ceiling as though counting. "…the middle of July."

"The first of August?" Sandy frowned. "That's not even nine months from now, my love. You must allow us time to…to…" He stuttered to a halt and stared at her.

Isabelle's cheeks heated to a boiling point.

"Isabelle? Are you…?" Sandy seemed to be unable to say the words.

"Yes, I am already in a family way, my love." She grinned at him and their mothers. It had been difficult, but she'd kept the news just for Christmas Day. "Last week I consulted with Mrs. MacGregor, the midwife in the village, and if all goes well, she says we should have our first wee bairn in our arms in mid-July."

"Oh, Isabelle, my love." Gently he enfolded her in his arms, making her feel so safe and so loved, as though she need worry about nothing else ever again. "How can I wait so long to see him or her? July is almost a year away."

"We must be patient, love." Isabelle grasped his arm and hugged him. "But then, that comes naturally to you, doesn't it Saint Sandy?"

"I am scarcely a saint, my love." He kissed her cheek, his eyes shining with love for her.

"I know a halo when I see one, my love," she whispered. "You have done nothing but show it to me ever since we met. It has been my saving grace up until now. And God willing, your light will continue to shine on us and our child, never to fade away."

The End

About the Author

Jenna Jaxon is a best-selling author of historical romance, writing in a variety of time periods because she believes that passion is timeless. She has been reading and writing historical romance since she was a teenager. A romantic herself, Jenna has always loved a dark side to the genre, a twist, suspense, a surprise. She tries to incorporate all these elements into her own stories.

She lives in Virginia with her family and a small menagerie of pets—including two vocal cats, one almost silent cat, two curious bunnies, and a Shar-pei mix named Frenchie.

Blog: www.jennajaxon.wordpress.com
Facebook: facebook.com/jenna.jaxon
Twitter: @Jenna_Jaxon
Instagram: passionistimeless
TikTok: @jennajaxon1

www.ingramcontent.com/pod-product-compliance
Lightning Source LLC
Chambersburg PA
CBHW070358200726
48294CB00003B/980

9781961275454